I CAN EXPLAIN...

AN AWKWARD LOVE NOVEL

MISSY JOHNSON

First Printing: Feb 2018
www.facebook.com/MissycJohnson

CHAPTER ONE
ALANA

"ALANA." Jade frowns, her skin almost cracking under the layers of makeup she has carefully piled onto her face. *Two guesses who she's trying to impress.* I chuckle to myself. "Are you listening to me?"

I snap back to attention and nod, still trying to hold back my smirk.

"Coffee. Dry cleaning. Take contracts over to Peterson Walker," I say, hoping I've gotten today's list right. It was the same as yesterday and the day before, so I'm pretty sure I'm safe.

"Right, well, just don't stuff it up this time, okay?" Jade sighs.

I bite my tongue before I say something that will probably end up getting me fired. You forget the sugar in the guy's coffee *one* time, and you suddenly have a reputation. Sure, that guy just happens to be Chase Winston, my arrogant, rude, adorably beautiful, attractive asshole of a boss, but still, it's not like I'm incapable of doing my job. Let's face it, half the things I'm asked to do, a monkey could do.

There was only one thing worse than being Chase Winston's personal assistant, and that's being one of the junior assistants who *answers* to his personal assistant. I'm simply here to make things easier for Jade and trust me when I say she takes full advantage of it. Well, I'm *guessing* it's worse because I've never had the pleasure of being his personal assistant. The guy never even acknowledges me.

I narrow my eyes at Peyton, who is hunched over her computer, trying not to laugh. I'm pretty sure watching me get my ass handed to me time and time again is the only thing keeping her working here. The second Jade leaves the office, I let loose with a string of obscenities under my breath.

"One time," I mumble, shaking my head. "I got it right yesterday, didn't I?"

"You've been working here how long?" Peyton giggles, her dark eyes sparkling with glee. I swear she lives for this shit. "You must've gotten that man a few hundred coffees. How on earth did you forget something like that?"

I blush. I know exactly how I forgot. I blame the sexy barista for making flirty eyes with me as the line slowly dwindled down until it was just him and me, standing at the counter, facing each other. I gently batted my eyelashes at him and gave him the sexiest smile I could muster, which was met with...nothing but a blank stare. So what if it turned out he was making flirty eyes with the dude behind me? I think my defense still stands.

"Never mind," I growl, rolling my eyes. "I better go do this before he pops an artery or something."

I fumble around on my desk for my purse and my keys, but all I can think about is how much I dislike my job. The only thing that makes it worthwhile is Peyton. Without her here to make the days bearable, I'd have left a long time ago. Well, that's not true. Peyton or not, I'd have stuck this out for as long as there was the tiniest hope of moving up into something more challenging.

I've been working at Winston Property Consultants (WPC) for nearly two years while I finished off my master's in statistics and business, which I'd *finally* graduated from two months ago. At twenty-four, and after nearly six years of school, all I have to show for it is this—a job that I'm way too overqualified for and hate more than life itself.

Why did I choose here? Because Chase Winston is the best, and I wanted to learn from the best. To put it simply, he merges struggling companies with stronger ones. He's kind of like the dating guru for businesses. I thought all I had to do was get my foot in the door and eventually, he'd notice my potential. Only now, I was beginning to wonder if it was worth the risk of not learning anything at *all*. I'm so hung up on working here that I could be harming any chance I have of doing anything within my chosen field. The longer I leave it, the harder it's going to be to explain why I stayed in this role for so long.

Right now, fresh out of college? I could easily find an entry level job with a dozen other companies that would advance me further than my current position ever would, but all of those firms were missing the one thing I wanted.

Chase. God, what can I say about Chase?

He's everything. Not only is he a self-made millionaire, but he's also hot, intimidating, sexy, smart, and a thousand other things that run through my head daily. My mind faces an ongoing struggle of hating him one minute and wanting to confess my love to him the next. I've never met anyone who can inspire and irritate me at the same time like Chase Winston can. And that's pretty impressive, considering I'm not even sure if he knows my name.

"Seriously, did you see the way she looked at me when she told me not to stuff it up?" I huff, stalking back over to Peyton. "Like, God forbid I put *two* sugars in his damn coffee instead of one. Hey, maybe I should slip some laxatives in there?" I say with an evil grin. "I mean, he walks around like he's got something lodged up his ass, maybe all he needs is a good, old-fashioned cleanout."

"Lanna—"

"No. I don't care how ridiculously sexy he is or how dreamy those blue eyes are to stare into," I say, cutting her off.

I was on a roll, and Peyton wasn't going to stop me. I have two years' worth of frustration to vent, and it's all coming out now, one way or another.

"He's an asshole to everyone here but Jade, and I bet that's only because she's sucking his cock. Not that *I* wouldn't go there if he asked me to—"

"*Lanna,*" Peyton hisses, her eyes wide.

"Oh, come on, like you wouldn't suck his cock too," I retort, nodding knowingly at her. "Hey, maybe we could tag team him."

We'd had a lengthy discussion about this a few weeks ago over a bottle of tequila, so I knew *exactly* what she wanted to do with that ten inches of pure stiff muscle. And I thought *I* was the dirty one. I chuckle to myself and turn around. My heart skips a beat when I spot Chase leaning against Jade's desk. He smirks at me and casually lifts one eyebrow.

Oh, god no.

My heart pounds as I wait for him to react. This can't be happening. *I cannot believe I just said that.* Well, I *can* believe it, because I say shit like that every day, but not when he's standing *right* behind me. I glare at Peyton, who releases a snort and then flushes, bowing her head. Chase's eyes don't leave me as I glance around the room, praying for an escape, but there isn't one.

It's like a scene from a really bad movie. With any luck, he'll drag me outside and throw me on the back of his bike and take me somewhere to have his way with me. Or his office will do just fine.

"Is Jade here?" he asks, directing his question at me, his smooth, deep voice making me shiver.

I shake my head, incapable of speaking. I think it's worse that he's ignoring the obvious issue of my outburst. I'd almost prefer for him to say something about it. Anything. *Almost...*

He nods, and then walks over to the door, stopping just as he reaches it. I brace myself as he turns his attention back to me.

"Alana?" he asks.

I force myself to meet his steel blue eyes, wishing he didn't find this so damn amusing.

"Yes?" I whisper, feeling sick. *God, I am so embarrassed.*

"While I appreciate your attentiveness to my health, I can *assure* you that *everything* is functioning just as it should. Maybe you should focus more on your job and less on things that don't concern you?" he asks lightly. "Like who *is* and *isn't* sucking my cock."

He walks out, briskly closing the door behind him.

I stumble over to my desk and slump down onto my chair, my eyes wide. I breathe out, feeling dazed. My heart's racing and I'm feeling a mixture of extreme nausea and embarrassment over the whole situation. Every time I think about what I just said, more or less to his *face*, I want to throw up.

Peyton rushes over to me, both panicked and trying not to laugh, which under any other circumstance would be a funny combination. I glare at her, which sets her off.

"I'm so sorry," she giggles, shaking her head. "I swear I'm not laughing at you, but that just made my fucking day."

"I'm glad I can be a source of amusement for you," I grumble, my tone sour.

"At least he knows your name now." she offers, her eyes twinkling.

I scowl at her. I think I preferred it when he didn't.

"I guess I really better go and do his stupid little list," I mutter.

I force myself to stand up, not sure whether to laugh or cry. It's already been the day from hell, and now I still have to go and complete his list? I should be glad to be escaping the office for a few hours because I'm already dreading the next time I have to face him.

Hopefully, I can manage to avoid him from now on.

CHAPTER TWO
ALANA

I THOUGHT DISTRACTING myself would be easy, but putting what just happened out of my head is proving to be harder than I thought. No matter how many times I force myself to think about something else, my mind always inevitably creeps back to that moment, and I relive the horror again.

I can't believe he was standing there that whole time and heard everything.

Driving the company car, I head toward the laundromat, sighing as I'm forced to slow to a stop in gridlocked traffic. It's always like this, which is one of the reasons I hate driving around here. I love inner city Boston most of the time, but having to go all the way over to the other side of town every few days to pick up his dry-cleaning was enough to send my nerves into a frenzy. Never mind the half a dozen dry-cleaners that are miles closer to the office. Some were even within *walking* distance. Hell, some even delivered to our *office* complex. That didn't matter because Chase has a boner for this place. *Probably because he didn't like the starch the other places used.*

I finally make it through the traffic and find a parking spot right out in the front of Grind, one of the few places where Chase accepted coffee from. Yes, I had a list of approved places to get his beverages from. You don't want to know what happens when I stray from that list. I detour inside and order his double shot latte, being extra careful to include his sugar, then I walk over the road to where the dry-cleaner is located.

Walking inside, I hand my ticket to the man behind the counter. He gives me a funny look and then disappears at the back while mumbling something under his breath. *Okay. That was strange.* I'm not sure what's going on, but I get the feeling it's not going to be good. I glance outside and frown. The longer this takes, the more traffic I'm going to hit on the way back, and the last thing I want is to give Chase any more reason to be annoyed at me.

I look back at the counter, relieved the attendant has returned with the owner in tow. Tony smiles at me, but he won't meet my eyes. I wait for him to tell me what the problem is. *Knowing my luck, his shirts are probably pink.*

"I'm sorry, Alana," Tony mumbles. "I don't know how to say this, but we're having trouble locating your order."

"Excuse me?" I say, my eyes widening. *No doubt this will be my fault too.* "How?"

Tony glances at the other guy. I come in here a lot, and I've never seen him before.

"Marcus only started this week." *Well, that explains that.* "He's still getting used to our regular clients, but he's pretty sure someone came in earlier today to collect it," Tony explains. He shakes his head. "I'm so sorry about this. Can you give us half an hour to fix this? Do you have something else you can do and then come back?"

What the hell was I going to do around here for half an hour, other than panic about losing my job? Look for another one? *Chase is going to kill me for this.* Work will be over by the time I get back. Okay, so that part didn't sound so bad, but still, I'm in enough trouble over what happened earlier. I glance down at the coffee in my hand and groan. I can already feel it going cold. I don't really have a choice other than to agree because going back without his dry-cleaning just isn't an option.

"Fine," I sigh. I scribble down my phone number and slide it across the counter. "Please call me and *not* Mr. Winston the moment you locate it," I say sternly. *He will freak if he finds out about this.*

Tony nods. "Of course. Again, I'm so sorry about this, Alana."

I smile tightly and then walk outside. I glance around, still not sure what to do to fill in the time. Then I wander across the road to the park and sit down under a large oak tree.

"Fuck," I growl, blinking back tears.

I swirl the coffee around in the cup and frown as it's delicious aroma engulfs me. My mouth waters as I stare at his precious coffee. *What the hell. It's going to be cold, anyway.* I may as well drink it and get him a fresh one on the way back, because going in there two hours late with no dry cleaning and a cold coffee would definitely get me fired. I set the empty cup down on the grass and wrap my arms around my chest, the breeze cooler than I was expecting.

I'm so upset with everything. I know I don't help the situation with scenarios like this morning, but I feel like I'm underappreciated and underutilized, and it's driving me insane. Sending me out to collect dry cleaning and get coffee when I'm qualified for so much more is so frustrating. Surely, there were better things I could be doing with my time. I didn't spend six years at college to do this, did I? Why am I even here? He's never going to give me a chance. Even more so now.

Maybe Dad is right. Maybe I am better off forgetting about Chase and making my mark somewhere else...

As if on cue, my phone vibrates loudly in my pocket. I pull it out, praying that it's Tony with good news and not Jade, wondering where the hell I am. It's neither, but I grin when I see Dad's name. I quickly answer it, eager to hear his voice.

"Hey," I say.

"How's my little girl?" Dad asks, his voice warm. I smile in spite of myself. Even though I'm not having a great day, talking to him always cheers me up.

"I'm okay," I say, trying to sound upbeat. Like always, he sees right through me.

"Are you sure about that?" Dad asks. "Because you sure as hell don't sound okay. Is it work again?"

I hesitate, not wanting to drag his mood down with mine.

"It's fine. I'm just having a rough day," I insist. "How are you?" I ask, changing the subject.

"Same as always. Doing too much, getting too old. You know how it is. Or, at least you will in about fifty years," he jokes, releasing one of his trademark, throaty laughs.

"Maybe you should retire, then?" I fire back at him.

It's a conversation we have every week, and he always promises that this year is going to be his last year of work. It never is, of course. I think part of him is afraid to give it up because it's such a huge part of his life. He's the kind of guy who always needs to be doing something, and if not work, then what? He's definitely not the lawn bowls or drinking at the club kind of guy, and it's not like he has a partner to occupy his time.

"Next year," he promises. I roll my eyes, even though he can't see me. "And I didn't call to talk about *me*. I called to check up on my girl. Work still a problem, I take it? Want me to come into your office and have a word with this Chase joker? I'll teach him a thing or two about how to treat people."

"God no," I mutter, wincing. *That would be brutal.* "Trust me. I'm fine. And it's Thursday already, which means it's practically the weekend," I add.

"Okay, if you say so... Can we catch up soon, then?" he asks. "So I can see for myself? And there's something I want to talk to you about, too."

"Sure," I say, with a frown. I don't like the way *that* sounds. Nothing good ever follows the words '*We need to talk.*' "How's Sunday for you?" I ask.

"Sunday sounds good. Text me the details," he says, making

me giggle. *As if he can even open a text.* "I'll let you get back to it. Love you, Lanni. Don't work too hard. And tell that boss of yours to shove off."

"I love you too," I say with a smile.

I hang up and settle back against the tree, taking the opportunity to close my eyes and just relax for a minute. I feel bad for not speaking to Dad more often, especially considering how close we are and the fact that we only have each other.

My mother died when I was only two. I don't remember much about her, other than what Dad told me. You get to the point where you're not sure what memories are real and what is just the result of him talking about her so often. If there was one thing he made sure of, it's that she wasn't forgotten. Even as a little girl, I could see how much he loved her. That love, imprinted in my mind, is a lot for any guy to live up to. Maybe that's why I struggle so much with relationships. *Or maybe it's just because I pick assholes.*

There were never any other women in the picture when it came to Dad. I don't know if that's because he never really moved on from Mom or because he didn't want me to have to deal with feeling like someone was taking her place. Still, I hate the idea of him being alone, especially since I'm moving on with my life and doing my own thing. If he just met someone, then I wouldn't have to worry about him so much. But, he's stubborn and set in his ways and no doubt impossible for any woman to live with. A few months ago, Peyton and I tried to set him up on a dating site for seniors. It didn't end well, partly because he's just so technologically challenged. He can barely manage to change the channel on a remote, let alone logging into a computer to check and reply to emails.

Still, he's my dad, and I wouldn't change a thing about him.

Finally, after what feels like hours, Tony calls.

"I'm sorry about all of this, Alana," he mutters. "But we've solved the mystery. Mr. Winston sent someone to collect his dry cleaning earlier today," he informs me, sounding pleased with himself. "I called him myself to confirm it."

What? He already had someone pick it up? I punch the ground next to me, annoyed. I close my eyes and will myself to stay calm because it's not just Chase I'm annoyed at. Tony called Chase after I *specifically* asked him not to?

"Fine," I say, clenching my teeth. "Thanks for letting me know."

I drag myself up from the ground and stalk back over to the café to order another coffee, tossing my empty cup in the trash along the way.

After battling even crazier traffic on the way back, I stumble into the office *just* before five, with what I'm sure is now a stone-cold coffee. I glance at the clock and curse under my breath. I've been gone for nearly two hours. My extreme absence hasn't gone unnoticed with Jade. She stares at me and just shakes her head like there are no words suitable to describe how incompetent she thinks I am. My anger rises because this is *not* my fault. If he'd fucking told me I didn't need to get his damn shirts, I could've walked the block down from the office to one of his *other* approved coffee providers. *I'm going to fucking kill him.*

Well, I would *if* I could work up the nerve to face him after what he heard me say this morning.

"Where are his shirts?" she hisses at me.

"He had someone else collect them this morning," I reply defensively, gritting my teeth.

She, of all people, should have known that. *It was probably her that went down to get them.* She looks confused, but then just shakes her head and storms back over to her desk. It's taking all my resolve not to follow her and tell her exactly what I think of her when her phone buzzes loudly on the desk. She snatches it up and lifts it to her ear, barking hello. She nods, scowling at me, and then carefully places the phone back on the receiver, before turning to me.

"Mr. Winston has requested that you bring him his coffee," she says stiffly. "Even though he was expecting you back more than *an* hour ago, he would still like to see you."

"Me?" I say, my mouth dropping open. I'm not sure I can face him right now without throwing his damn drink in his face. I'm still livid that he wasted half my day. "Why?"

"God, I don't know. What am I, his keeper?" Jade snaps.

"Well, yeah, I kind of thought you were," I say sweetly.

She narrows her eyes at me and grits her teeth, looking like she's seconds away from exploding. I know I'm baiting her, but at this point, I just don't care anymore. This is by far the worst day I've ever had, and antagonizing Jade is just making it all a *little* bit brighter.

"Would you just take the damn coffee in so that we can all go home?" she huffs, throwing her arms up in annoyance.

Shaking my head, I storm out the door and across the hallway to Chase's office. Five seconds ago, I was full of fire and ready to march in there and defend myself, but all that confidence has gone out the window, leaving me a quivering mess.

All I can think about is what happened this morning and what he must think of me. *Get it over with.* I take a deep breath and force myself into at least pretending I'm calm before I knock three times. My hands shake as I wait for him to answer.

"Are you going to stand out there all evening or come inside?" He eventually calls out to me. I wince as I catch the hint of irritation in his voice.

I turn the handle and take another deep breath as I push the door open and walk inside. I let go, jumping as the door closes with a loud bang. I'm clutching his coffee so tightly that I'm afraid I'm going to drop it, but somehow, I manage to hold my head up high.

"Your coffee," I say, walking toward him.

I look him right in the eye, even though I feel like I'm about to trip over my heels at any moment. He glares at me, and I glare right back, hoping I look more collected than I really am because inside, I'm pretty sure I'm about to shit myself. I set the cup down on his desk and step back, placing my hands behind my back so he can't see how tightly they're clenched.

"No dry cleaning?" he asks, lifting his eyebrows.

I frown when I see the tiniest smirk on his lips. *God, I want nothing more than to slap that smirk clean off those lips.* He reaches for his coffee and examines it, then returns to staring at me.

"Thank you for the beverage," he adds, "I don't recall requesting an *iced* coffee, but I guess it's better than nothing, right?" He raises his eyebrows when I don't answer.

"I guess," I mutter, finding my voice.

"So," he says, glancing at me again. "Is there a reason you're not weighed down with my freshly pressed shirts?"

He takes the lid off the cup and frowns as he examines the contents. I stand there, my anger growing by the second. Seriously? What the hell does he think I've done? Tried to poison him?

"What, are you checking for those laxatives?" I snap, creasing my eyebrows. "And I'm not weighed down with your shirts because you already *had* someone else pick them up, remember?"

"Oh. Right," he says, nodding slowly, a glint in his eye. "My mistake. I guess it slipped my mind. And as for whether I think you may have tampered with my drink?" He shrugs, his eyes gleaming. "After this morning, why would I trust you at all?" He holds the cup out to me. "Do me a favor? Take a sip."

"Are you serious?" I ask him with a laugh. Then I frown because I'm not sure whether to take it from his hands or not. "You *really* believe that I might have drugged it?"

"No. I just get off on watching women drink my coffee," he retorts in a deadpan tone.

"Fine," I sigh.

If it will shut him up. I snatch the cup from his hands and gulp down half its contents. Smiling at him, I hand it back. He frowns when he sees most of his coffee is gone.

"Satisfied?" I ask sweetly.

"Almost," he murmurs. He motions to the chair on the other side of his desk. "Sit down," he commands. I do as I'm told, still cringing over earlier and not sure what he wants with me now, other than to embarrass me further.

"Are you happy working here, Alana?" he asks.

He shifts forward in his seat and runs his hand over the light stubble covering his jawline, which sends a shiver down my spine. *What I wouldn't give to be the one running my hand over that.* God, I can feel my nipples hardening at the thought.

I stare at him, remembering he just asked me a question. His eyes are serious like he's given this a lot of thought. I don't care how unhappy I might seem, I never expected him to be the person who noticed. I hesitate, not sure whether to be honest with him about this or not.

What have I got to lose?

At this point, I'm probably a couple of sentences away from being fired anyway.

"I'm happy," I say, choosing my words carefully. "I just wish you would give me more responsibility. All I seem to do is fetch your coffee and collect your dry cleaning—"

"You returned without my shirts and with a cold coffee," he reminded me.

"Neither of which were my fault," I say defensively. "You

had someone else pick them up already. You sent me out chasing my tail around for no other reason than to amuse yourself."

"Well, that's not entirely true," he murmurs, his lips creeping into a grin. "How else would I have gotten this delicious coffee?" I narrow my eyes at him, and his smirk widens. "Alana, have you read the job description for your role? If anything, letting you handle the responsibility of fetching my coffee is a step up."

"You're an asshole, you know that?" I say, not bothering to hide my annoyance any longer. I'm about five promotions overqualified for the role I'm in now, and he knows it. "Fire me, don't fire me, I don't care. But I'm not going to sit here and let you walk all over me."

"Okay, the dry cleaning *was* just an innocent mistake on my part," he replies, folding his arms across his chest. "But how can I give you more responsibility when you've repeatedly shown me that you can't even get the simplest of tasks right?" he asks. He picks up his cup and drinks the rest of his coffee. "Like my coffee, for example."

"Excluding today, *one* time in probably three or four hundred coffees, I've forgotten to get your goddamn sugar, and *that's* your reasoning behind not recognizing what I can do?" I practically shout. Tears sting my eyes, but I won't give him the satisfaction of seeing me cry.

Breath, Alana. Don't let him win this.

My fingers fidget in my lap as I try to control my tears. I do not want to lose my grip in front of him because it's exactly what he wants. All I want to do is get out of there because this guy is a psychopath.

"Was there anything else you wanted me for?" I ask, my voice cold. "Because I have an appointment to get to."

"An appointment?" he asks in his most patronizing tone. "Well, I wouldn't want to keep you from something so important," he murmurs.

I glower at him, wanting nothing more than to punch the sparkle out of his eyes.

"You're free to go, Alana, but I think we should schedule a performance review so we can discuss our issues in greater detail," he says. He sits back in his chair and smirks at me. "Say, next week?"

I nod, trying not get flustered under his intense stare.

"Thank you," I mutter, even though I still think he's the one in the wrong.

I stand and walk over to the door, aware that his eyes are still on me. I shiver and walk out, refusing to look back. I only let myself relax once I'm safely back in my office and that door is shut. *Thank god everyone else has already gone.* I walk over to my cubical and slump into my chair, planting my head face down on the desk.

Holy shit, that was intense.

What a giant asshole. Adrenaline surges through my body, and all I want to do is scream. After that, I have a sudden newfound respect for Jade. I have no idea how she manages to put up with him day after day.

Hell, I struggled with the last five minutes.

CHAPTER THREE
CHASE

I WATCH her thoughtfully as she leaves my office, my eyes falling on her ass as she sashays across my floor. Does she know how sexy she looks in that skirt? Never mind the fact that it's a modest length at almost to her knee, it's so fucking tight that it just clings to her curves, making her ass look like it's ready to burst out. Then there's that creamy white shirt that's just sheer enough to give me the slightest glimpse of her bra. I sit forward as she closes the door, trying to control my erection, but it's no use.

I glance at my phone. It's after five, so technically I'm done for the day, so I see no reason not to relieve a little tension. In my defense, I'm not in the habit of yanking it out at work and going to town on myself, but today has been a shit of a day. One I want to try and forget about any way I can.

"At least it's nearly fucking over," I mutter to myself.

Reaching down, I lower my zipper, sliding my fingers

around my length and letting it bounce free. With a groan, I lean back in my chair and pump my fist along my shaft, imagining Alana on her knees in front of me, taking my length into her mouth. The whole time I was talking to her, all I could focus on was those pouty, red lips.

Alana. I shake my head and smile as my fingers work my dick. Until today, I thought her name was Melissa. In fact, I'm pretty sure I called her that a few times. Alana suits her so much better.

Hearing her say those things about me in her office, listening to her talk about my cock like that, made me hard as fuck. I'd gotten nothing done all day because all I could think about was her. And just now, the way she stood up to me? Major turn-on.

I am so sick of women telling me what they *think* I want to hear and then just falling to their knees, ready to do whatever I ask of them. That had been Jade in a nutshell. Her second day here, her mouth was on the end of my cock, whether I wanted it or not. It was fine for a while, but I got bored like I always do. I needed a challenge. Something to distract me, someone, where there's no risk of feelings developing, because inevitably, that's what always ruins things for me. My requirements definitely were not something that any woman I associated with could satisfy. Hell, I wasn't even sure Alana was up to the challenge, but at least she showed potential.

I block all thoughts of everything except Alana out of my head as my orgasm builds. I groan, stroking my cock, while my other hand wraps around the edge of the desk. I lever myself forward, my throat constricting as I come.

"Fuck," I hiss. My fists tightens around my girth as I release, groaning as I come hard into my hand.

Breathing heavily, I clean myself up, thankful that Alana had the foresight to bring me extra napkins with my coffee. *She must've known I'd be whacking off to her the moment she left me alone.* Hell, if I thought I could get away with it, I'd have done it with her sitting right there.

Breathing hard, I tuck myself back in and buckle up my pants, just as someone pounds on my door. I jump up, thanking God they weren't just a few minutes earlier, or that would've really ruined my day.

"Yes," I growl.

The door swings open. I look up and double take when I see Josh walking toward me. *Holy shit. I came so hard I'm seeing things.* But no, he's really there, smiling at me like we're old friends. He sits down.

"Chase. How are you?"

He asks like it hasn't been nearly two years since I last saw him. He almost has me fooled that he doesn't care how I'm going to react, but the look in his eyes gives him up. *He's terrified.* Just as he fucking should be. I sit back in my chair and frown at him, not saying a word.

"Josh," I say, my tone stiffer than my dick had been only minutes before. "I can say with all honesty that you're the *last* person I expected to walk into my office tonight."

"Chase..." He sighs as I lift my eyebrows. He at least has

the decency to look ashamed, though not keeping in contact is pretty low on the list of shit my brother has done to me. "I've been wanting to call you. I've just been so busy with work and stuff," he mumbles.

"Stuff being my ex-wife?" I ask, an edge in my voice. "How *is* Casey, by the way?"

"She's fine," Josh replies. To his credit, he's not letting me bait him into an argument. "You're not going to make this easy for me, are you?" he asks, studying me.

"*Should* I be making this easy for you, Josh?" I ask, keeping my voice calm.

The funniest thing about all of this is that he's oblivious to what today is. At least I *hope* he is because turning up in my office, on my wedding anniversary is a bit of a cunt move.

"Considering the circumstances, yes," he replies, answering my question. He stands and wanders over to the window. "Playing the victim doesn't suit you, Chase. You were just as much in the wrong as we were. Maybe even more so." He frowns and turns to face me. "Anyway, I'm not here to dig up the past."

"Really," I say. I watch him suspiciously because I'm not sure I believe that. "So why *are* you here, then?"

He hesitates and then turns away again. I sigh, because all I want to do is shake answers out of him. Why can't he just get it out? Say what he has to say and then fuck off?

"Hey, do you want to go out somewhere? Get a drink?" he suddenly asks. "They're playing some live music down at The Jazz Bar. Maybe we could head there, for old times' sake?"

A drink?

I swallow a laugh, and then shrug, pretending that him turning up after all this time hasn't brought back a whole heap of painful memories. Things I thought I'd forgotten, or at least, moved on from. I want to kick him out, but on the other hand, I don't want him to see how much his impromptu visit is getting to me. *If a drink is all I need to do for him to leave me alone for another two years, then I'll take it.*

"Sure," I finally say. "Let's go."

NEITHER OF US says much as he drives us over to the bar. I glance out the window of his Merc—ironically, the same one I caught him fucking my wife in—pretending I give a damn about whatever it is he has to say. *But I do care, don't I?* I'm so conflicted, because as much as I hate what he did to me, he's still my brother. And my only living family member.

"How's work?" he asks, attempting small talk.

"Busy," I murmur.

He takes the hint and stops trying to engage me in bullshit, pointless small talk. Both of us remain silent the rest of the drive until we pull into the parking lot behind the bar. We get out and walk inside. I'm impressed to see that not much has changed, and it's still the quiet little place that I remember. It's located on the far side of town, so not many people know about it. Especially since there's been a big influx of trendy bars closer to the city. Little places like this had been overlooked, and although it sucked for them from a business sense, it suited me down to the ground. I hate crowds almost as much as I hate socializing.

We find ourselves a table. I order a scotch while Josh orders a beer. Catch-ups like this used to be a regular thing and something that I looked forward to, but they haven't happened in a long time. We used to hit this very place nearly every weekend, but that was before life and work became more important than family. Before everything went to shit with Casey.

A break-up is messy enough, but when your brother falls in love with your wife, it jumps to a whole new level of complicated.

"So, what's going on?" I ask, taking a sip of my drink.

I've already decided that I'm not going to like whatever it is he has to tell me. It's got to be big, or he wouldn't be here. He's either dying, or he's getting married. I'm not sure which piece of news will upset me more.

"Not much. Same old shit, different day, really." He frowns and studies the surface of the table, running his finger repeatedly over it a tiny crack in the wood. I'm almost at the point where I want to reach over and snap it off. "I just wanted to catch up because I feel like we lost contact when—"

"When you stole my wife from me?" I supply.

He glares at me. "You know as well as I do that things aren't that black and white," he growls. His eyes flash, daring me to dispute that. Then he sighs and presses his palms flat down on the table, as though he just remembered there's a reason he's here.

"Since you brought Casey up...I did want to talk to you

about something..." I raise my eyebrows as he hesitates. The poor guy looks like he's about to pass out. "We're getting married."

"You're getting *married*?" I repeat, my voice sounding much calmer than I feel. Josh stares at me, looking for any hint of how I'm digesting his news, but I'm a master of disguising my emotions. "Congratulations."

"Do you actually mean that?" he asks with uncertainty.

"Why wouldn't I?" I say with a shrug. I stare him right in the eye until he breaks contact.

"Chase, I know that you said that you were fine with us being together, but I just wanted to make sure you meant that," he mumbles. He lifts his beer to his mouth and drinks half of it in one go.

Yep. He's definitely panicking.

"Of course I meant it," I snap. "Why wouldn't I want the two of you happy? Just because Casey is the only woman I've ever loved, and my only brother stole her from my arms. Why would that make a difference?"

"Chase, you know it wasn't like that, don't you?" He sounds frustrated now, which makes me happy.

"Like what?" I ask innocently, pretending that I have no idea what he's talking about.

"You were *cheating* on her, dammit," he growls, his expression darkening. A little part of me feels like I've won, seeing him snap like that. "I know that doesn't excuse me for falling in love with her, but it at least blurs the lines a *little* my way, right?" he asks.

"I'm glad she's happy, and I'm glad you're the one who's making her happy," I say, ignoring the weight of Josh's stare. I rub the bridge of my nose and then I force myself to smile at him, because that couldn't have sounded less sincere if I'd tried. He sighs and bows his head, probably realizing that it's probably the best response he's going to get from me. I sigh and try to swallow my pride.

"So, when is the wedding?" I ask.

Josh's eyes cast downwards. "It's in three weeks."

I cough and raise my hand to my mouth, sputtering my drink into my clenched fist.

"Three weeks? That's an awfully short engagement," I say with a growl.

"Not really. We've, uh, we've been engaged for about six months," he mumbles, not meeting my eyes.

I snort. He's spent more time looking at the floor than *me* since we got here, which just about sums up this whole night.

"And you're only now getting around to telling me?" I ask, scowling at him.

I don't know whether to be amused or pissed, but being cut out of his life hurts more than I thought it would.

"Am I even invited to this wedding, Josh?" I ask him.

"Of course you are," he snaps. "Why do you think I'm here?"

"But I wasn't invited a week ago, was I?" I press. "Or didn't you think I'd need the six months' notice your other guests received. Because, you know, I sit on my ass all day and do nothing. What the hell do I need time to plan for?"

"No, I..." He sighs and sits back in his chair. "You want me to be honest with you? No. you weren't invited last week because, until today, Case didn't want you there."

"Then, what's changed?" I ask.

"She realized how much *I* want you there," he says quietly.

"Well, if *you* want me there, how could I possibly refuse?" I say dryly.

I bite my tongue and back down from the conversation like I always do when it comes to Josh. Because no matter what happens, he'll always be my baby brother. If the choice had been mine, we wouldn't have lost contact like we did, because we're the only family each other have. Josh pauses long enough to raise his eyes to mine. Anxiety flashes through them.

"So? Will you come?" he asks quietly.

"I'll be there," I say, after a brief pause. "You know I'll fucking be there."

I remember the day our parents died like it was yesterday, even though it was twenty years ago. I was nine, and Josh was only five. When they told me that they'd been killed in a car accident on the way to our school, I didn't cry. Instead, I wrapped my arms around Josh and told him everything was going to be fine. I knew I had to be the man and protect my little brother. I had no idea what was going to happen to us, but I couldn't let him know that.

That night, I wrapped my arms around his shoulders and held him in his bed as he cried. I promised him that no matter what, I'd always be there for him. I'd never let him feel alone.

I made a promise once. I'm not about to break it.

"There's, uh, one more thing," he finally mumbles.

"What now?" I ask with an exasperated sigh. I shift in my seat, feeling restless.

"You can tell me to go to hell, but I want to know if you'd be my best man." He winces as he forces the words out, like he's sure they're going to be the ones that break me.

"At your *wedding*?" I say with a laugh. "It's not enough that you've given me three weeks' notice after not hearing from you in two years. *Or* that you're marrying my ex-wife?"

"Sorry, I shouldn't have even asked you," Josh mutters.

"No. It's fine," I say. I sigh and rub the back of my neck. "If that's what it takes to convince you that I'm okay with you two getting married, then fine."

I finish my drink and then stand up, pushing my chair back in.

"I better get home. It's been a long day, and I have even more on for tomorrow."

"Okay, I'll be in touch. And Chase?" He pauses, his dark eyes meeting mine. "Thanks for this. It means a lot to me."

"No problem," I say as I stare into his eyes. "Though next time you ask for my blessing to marry my ex-wife, maybe make sure it's not on our damn wedding anniversary?"

I STALK out before he can answer, leaving him to ponder that.

It's a good twenty minutes from the bar to my place, but I decide to walk and catch a cab to work tomorrow. I figure I can use the time to think and clear my head. It has nothing to do with the fact that I know all I'll be thinking about when I get back to my large, empty apartment is how alone I really am.

"Fuck," I hiss, running my hands through my hair.

A passing woman gives me a wide berth and tightens her grip on her purse as she walks by me. I laugh because now I'm that strange guy in the street who nobody wants to be near.

Tonight was strangely reminiscent of the same night three years ago. *Our last anniversary together, which I spent alone, walking home from a bar, just like this.* Only back then, it was much later and I was so drunk, I could barely walk.

How the fuck did things get so messed up?

I met Casey in my second year of college. I pretty much knew right away that she was someone I wanted to be with. I couldn't resist that long, blonde hair or the way her steel blue eyes felt like they were ripping through my soul every time she looked at me. She had me wrapped around her finger from pretty much the word go, and she damn well knew it.

Early on in our relationship, I was the perfect boyfriend. But as my studies became more demanding, she had to share my attention, something she didn't take very well. She'd get frustrated at me for working too late into the night or for forgetting the one month anniversary of our first date. Or missing a dinner reservation because I put all my time and energy into my studies.

I was ambitious and determined to make something of my life, and I wasn't going to let anything get in the way of that. Not even Casey. I loved her. I loved her more than anything, but I struggled to show her that. Still, I persevered. I wanted to give her the life she deserved, and I wanted to show Josh that *anything* was achievable if you worked hard enough for it.

That's kind of funny, considering he ended up with my wife.

When we left college and got married, things were better for a while, but once I found my place in the business world, that quickly began to change. Just like college, I put everything into getting to where I am now, and I sacrificed my marriage in the process. I regret that every day. More than anyone knows. Especially Josh.

Josh thinks he knows everything that happened between Casey and me, but he doesn't know the half of it. Not that I'll ever tell him, because if he found out the truth, it would crush him. As much as I'm hurting, I don't want my brother to suffer. I just want him to be happy.

"Fuck. I'm such a pussy," I mutter to myself.

I shake my head at what a mess I am. I have every part of my life in place, *except* when it comes to the one thing I want. People assume that I'm this hard, intimidating guy who only cares about himself because that's what I want them to think. The truth is, I'm not. I'm the guy who's jealous of his own brother because he's managed to achieve what I couldn't.

Putting Casey first.

I ARRIVE BACK at my apartment and toss my keys down on the counter as I pass through the kitchen. Peeling off my clothes, I stumble down to the bathroom and turn on the shower. I'm not that drunk, but I can barely keep my eyes open as I stand under the thick stream of water.

Turning off the taps, I step out and wrap the towel around my waist, then walk down to my bedroom. I quickly dry myself off and then climb onto the bed, collapsing face down into my pillows. I roll over and stare at the ceiling, too exhausted to bother covering myself up. As tired as I am, I can't switch my mind off.

What a fucking day. Learning about Josh and Casey really topped it off. The only highlight was learning that the assistant to my assistant wants to suck my cock.

CHAPTER FOUR
ALANA

I WILL NOT EMBARRASS myself today.

I figure if I say it enough, I'll actually start to believe it.

I march through the revolving doors that lead into the office complex, a good ten minutes early. It's something I don't think I've done in my entire life because getting in on time is usually a struggle in itself. I'm feeling pretty good about myself because today is a new day. And then I remember that this is Chase, and I'm me. No doubt I'll give him plenty of other reasons to fire me before five o'clock hits. *At least he can't be on my back for being late.* Then again, I haven't made it up to the office yet. I still had time to ruin this.

I impatiently press the button for the elevator, as if hitting it fifteen times is going to hurry the damn thing up. The doors eventually open and I step into the empty car and wait for the doors to close again. They're just starting to creak shut when a hand appears out of nowhere, forcing them back open. I sigh because I was hoping to avoid small talk with someone I wasn't really interested in chatting with. I keep my eyes on my phone, hoping I look too busy to interrupt.

"I'm going to assume you haven't realized that it's me, because ignoring your boss like this could be considered *very* rude."

I freeze. That voice. *Chase.*

For a second, I contemplate fleeing, but it's four stupid levels. If I can't handle being in his presence for *that* short a time, I have no business being here at all.

"Sorry, I was busy with..."

My voice trails off, because admitting I'm trawling Facebook just feels wrong. He smirks at me, obviously enjoying my discomfort. This guy thrives on seeing me squirm and not in a good way. I hunch down and study my phone, so he can't see the color rise up to my cheeks.

"Facebook?" he questions. I look up to find him peering over my shoulder. "If you're finding yourself with too much spare time, I'd be happy to provide you with something to fill that space," he murmurs.

I cringe and shove my phone back in my bag—the thought of him filling any space of mine is way too much.

"Thanks for the offer, but I think I'm okay," I manage to reply.

My heart pounds in my chest as I stare straight ahead at the door. I'm trying to not focus on the sound of his breathing, but it's hard when he insists on standing so close to me. Then, out of nowhere, his fingers are touching my waist. I jump and turn around to glare at him.

"Sorry, I lost my footing and stumbled right into you there for a second," he says innocently. I frown because I can't tell if he's serious or not. "Don't worry, Alana, I'm not going to bite," he promises. His eyes shine as he adds, "That is, unless you want me to."

My knees shake. I'm frozen on the spot and unable to move as my heart pounds out of control. The worst part is, the idea of him biting me or doing *anything* at all is turning me on to no end. My heart is beating so loud that I'm sure he can hear it. I step to the side, so I'm standing against the wall, not comfortable with being in front of him. Not because I don't trust him, but because the idea of him looking at me is making me anxious.

"Are you okay?" he asks, his eyes sparkling. "You're looking a bit pale."

"I'm fine," I say, forcing a smile.

I watch the levels as they slowly go up, one by one. It pauses on level three for what feels like forever, before we finally reach our floor. I shift impatiently, waiting for the doors to open, but they don't. After a while, I start to panic, resisting the urge to step forward and start banging the shit out of the buttons to get this thing moving again.

"For some reason, this particular elevator always seems to pause on level four for ages before the doors open," Chase muses. "Have you noticed that?"

"I'm certainly noticing it now," I mutter, my heart skipping a beat. "You'd think management might look into something like that if they were aware of it," I snap.

God, I'm beginning to sweat. I swallow, trying to loosen my collar.

He chuckles, his eyes twinkling with amusement. "You're right. Management here really sucks, huh? You're quite high strung when you're stressed, Alana. Have you have ever thought of doing something to help you relax?"

My head jerks around, and I flush, wondering what that's supposed to mean.

"What exactly are you suggesting?" I growl.

He shrugs, that sexy smirk never leaving his lips. "I don't know. Like meditation...or something," he says.

I scoff. The look in his eyes tells me he means *anything* but meditation.

"Thanks, but I'm not really into that new age crap," I retort, glancing at the door.

"Then what are you into, Alana?" he asks. "Do you prefer to employ more proven strategies for relaxation?"

I'm starting to feel sick, but I manage to glare at him as I try and think of a witty response. I panic when one doesn't come, but I'm saved by the doors finally deciding to open. With a great big sigh of relief, I practically fall out of the elevator and onto my knees. He walks around me slowly, so he's standing in front of me. I get to my feet, not daring to look him in the eye.

"I'm late for work," I mumble, before making my escape.

"You do realize that I'm your boss?" he calls out to me as I bolt down the hallway. "I don't think it counts as being late for work when you're late because you're talking to me."

I ignore him, even though he makes an excellent point and stumble into my office. I slam the door shut behind me, my heart racing. Peyton looks up from her computer with a frown.

"Are you okay?" she asks. I glance over to where Jade sits at her desk and nod.

"Fine," I mumble.

I'm feeling anything but fine, but I don't want to air my problems in front of Jade. I drag my chair forward and focus on the stack of files that Jade has generously dumped on my desk.

I struggle to focus at first, but it isn't long before I'm distracted away from my issues by mergers and reports that need updating in the system. I'm so lost in my own little world that I don't even notice when Chase walks in, until he's standing in front of my desk, staring down at me.

"I need to borrow Alana for the day," he announces to Jade, his eyes on me.

"What?" I squeak. My eyes widen almost as far as Jade's.

He nods briskly. "I have to go and iron out some issues with the Phillip Trung merger, and I need someone there to take notes for me."

Probably because he never got his pen license. I stifle a laugh.

"Peyton is faster at writing shorthand than her." Jade frowns.

"That's wonderful, but I've requested Alana." Chase frowns at Jade. "Do you have a problem with that?"

"No," she replies, her voice soft.

I sit there, expecting him to say something else, when it becomes obvious he's waiting for me. I jump up, gather my things together and toss them in my bag. My heart pounds as I follow him out the door. I don't even trust myself to look at Peyton, who I can feel staring at me. Mainly because I don't trust her not to give me a high five or something equally as obvious.

The ride down in the elevator to the basement is quiet. He's busy reading something on his phone, and I'm doing my best to pretend I'm immersed in something myself. In reality, all I'm doing is staring at the blank screen on my phone, praying that A, I don't make an idiot of myself, and B, the elevator doesn't stop randomly again. I breathe out when the doors slide open and reveal the basement.

I follow him over to his car. It looks expensive, but it's not as flashy as I was expecting. He clicks a button on his keys and unlocks the door, starting the ignition before we're even in it. Mildly impressed, I open the passenger side and slide inside, clicking my seat belt into place. I clasp my hands in my lap, my nerves kicking up a gear at the idea of being in the same car as him. I have no idea what to say, so I stare out the window, my body tensing as he slides in beside me.

"Are you ready?" he asks.

He flashes me a smile that makes my knees tremble. *Thank god I'm sitting down.*

I nod. I'm still not exactly sure why he needs me to go with him, but I know better than to air my confusion in front of him.

He fumbles on the back seat and retrieves a thick folder, tossing it on my lap. I glance down at what I'm holding, a shiver of excitement racing through me. Not many people would get excited about statistics and numbers, but I'm definitely one of them. Forget flowers and chocolates; hand me a folder full of statistics, and I'm all yours.

I don't know much about the merger between Trung and Einswing because as a junior assistant, the closest I've come to seeing the file is when I'm entering information into my computer. I'd been following it in the media, so I knew enough to know that the amount of money this merger was going to bring to the company would come close to matching every other client combined.

This merger was huge, and I'm excited to be sitting in on *any* part of it. At this point, I don't care what his motivations are.

"Have a read-through and tell me what you think," he says.

You don't need to tell me twice. I dive in, aware that he's watching me.

"You actually find this stuff interesting, don't you?" he remarks, his lips twitching.

"Don't you?" I reply, glancing back down at the folder on my lap. "A lot of this just comes down to numbers and how far is Einswing willing to compromise to stay afloat. All you needed to do was find something they have to offer to use as bait to get the attention of a competitor. Like Trung," I conclude.

Chase smiles at me, and I swear I see a flash of admiration in his eyes.

"You know your shit," he acknowledges.

I flush. "This kind of thing fascinates me," I say with an embarrassed shrug. "Math and statistics have always been my kind of thing because everything always comes down to numbers."

"Well, maybe not *everything*," he teases. I blush furiously, which makes him chuckle even more. "What did you study in college?"

"I majored in statistics and minored in business," I say proudly.

"And you're my junior assistant?" he says with a low whistle. "A little over qualified, wouldn't you say?"

I shrug. *Finally, he's noticing me.*

"My degree is definitely something I hope to have to use one day. I'd really love to challenge myself."

I still remember as a little kid going over complex math problems with my dad. I was always a few years ahead of the other kids in class, which meant I was quickly bored with the syllabus. School just didn't motivate me enough, so Dad did his best to help out. In my junior year, I was passing exams meant for sophomore college students.

"What did you say this meeting was for?" I ask with a frown, forcing myself to focus back on the notes in front of me.

Admittedly, I'm no expert, but it looks like this merger is all but complete. I certainly can't see anything that would require bringing me along to take notes. In fact, I can't even see a reason as to why Chase would need to be here. I struggle to believe that he attended *all* the closures for his mergers. *Maybe just the ones he wants to impress me with.*

"I didn't," he grins. "I just like to keep my hands in things. I like making sure I'm aware of *everything* that's happening around me."

The idea of his hands anywhere near me makes me shiver. Why bring me along, then? Is this all just his way of messing with me? I flush. Could he be any more self-centered? Like he would waste an entire day of his busy schedule just to mess with me. *Stop being so ridiculous and just use this as a chance to learn.* And with any luck, I'll be able to show Chase Winston what I'm capable of.

Twenty minutes later, we park in front of Trung Enterprises. I climb out, smoothing out my skirt whilst juggling my bag and the thick folder of notes. I follow Chase inside, watching with interest how everyone we pass acknowledges him. It's like being out with a celebrity. I'm not used to seeing people act like this around him. At work, people are scared of him. He has a reputation for being hard and fearless, but all I see here is admiration and appreciation.

My extensive late-night googling on Chase had informed me that he lost both parents when he was very young, leaving him and his brother in the care of an aunt. The day he turned twenty-one, he invested nearly his entire, modest inheritance into his business, and then he slowly built it from the ground up. If that didn't spell guts, I don't know what did.

Chase was no trust fund baby. He learned everything he could about business and making money so he could secure a future for himself. How can you feel anything other than admiration for someone with that kind of dedication?

We walk into the conference room, and I stand back so I can observe Chase as he works the room. He shakes hand after hand, as people acknowledge him with warmth. An attractive blonde woman looks up, her face lighting up when she realizes who it is. My stomach clenches as I pretend not to listen to their conversation.

"You were supposed to call me," she murmurs, a playful frown on her face.

"No, *you* suggested I call you. I never said I would," he replies, his lips twitching into a grin. "On the other hand, I never said I *wouldn't...*"

"You still have my number," she says lightly. "And I still have those handcuffs if you're interested."

Chase looks up, his eyes meeting mine. I gasp when I realize that I was staring at them. He raises his eyebrows slightly, making me blush furiously. I drop my gaze, my heart racing.

"Are you going to stand over there the whole meeting or sit down?" he asks, patting the seat next to him.

I nod and walk over to the table, smiling at his friend as I slide onto my seat. She nods back, but it's cold and forced. Before she can say anything, the door opens, and a man walks in wearing an expensive, yet very flamboyant, suit. I immediately recognize him as Phillip Trung from the numerous television interviews he'd done over the last few weeks.

"Mr. Winston," he says, sounding shocked to see Chase. "This is a nice surprise. Unless you're here with a problem? In which case, I'd wish you death."

Chase chuckles. "Wonderful to see you, too, Phillip. Everything is going according to plan. I'm just here to ensure things stay that way," Chase assures him. "You've got nothing to worry about. You're acquiring a strong company with a solid work ethic."

"Lovely." Phillip nods. He glances at me, intrigued. "Though you know I only care about the numbers. And I see you brought company."

"My assistant, Alana Morrison. Alana, this is one of the most powerful men you'll ever meet, Phillip Trung," Chase says.

"Oh, stop schmoozing me, Mr. Winston," Phillip chuckles. "And if you want to kiss my ass, get in line behind all of these lovely people."

He sits down so the meeting can begin. I watch with interest, a flutter of excitement racing through me as the contracts are exchanged and signed. It's all over in a matter of minutes, leaving me wondering once again why he brought me all the way over here. I get to my feet, along with Chase and everyone else.

Phillip walks over to Chases and enthusiastically lifts him

into a hug. I cover my mouth to hide my amusement because poor Chase looks lost in Phillip's overzealous embrace.

"Thanks again for coming out, even though it clearly wasn't necessary," Phillip says.

"A true businessman stays ahead of the problem; he doesn't chase it," Chase replies, a twinkle in his eye. "I'd much rather waste my day and know that my biggest client is happy than to sit back and wait for something to go wrong." He puts out his hand, which Phillip takes in a firm handshake. "I'll be in touch."

I follow Chase out the door, listening to him whistle as he saunters down the hallway. As we walk outside and into the bright sunshine, I ponder over his words, half believing what he said in there.

Maybe this wasn't about me at all, and he really does just care about his clients.

"You really do go above and beyond for your clients, don't you?" I say, eyeing him thoughtfully.

"You mean what I said in there?" Chase laughs as he glances back at me. "I told him what he wanted to hear. I had that merger sewn so tight that there was no way anything was going to go wrong."

"Then why are we here?" I ask, confused.

Nearly the whole day is gone and I'm struggling to comprehend what the point was, if not to keep Phillip happy.

"I just wanted to prove that I'm in control," he says simply. "And that if I want something, I get it." He glances at his phone and curses. "*Fuck*. I'm sorry, Alana, but I didn't realize it was so late. I have a meeting to get to. Would you mind catching a cab back to the office?" He reaches into his pocket for his wallet and retrieves a credit card. "I'll pay, of course."

"Sure," I say, shocked and slightly relieved that I don't have to travel back with him.

"Thanks," he mutters. "I owe you one."

CHAPTER FIVE
ALANA

IT'S way after five when I get back to the office, and not surprisingly, everyone else has already left. All I want to do is head home and relax, but I feel bad, because it's Friday, and I haven't been to the gym all week. Besides, burning off some of this tension that seems to be clinging to me isn't the worst idea in the world.

I check my phone and see a few messages from Peyton. I call her to see what she's up to, since she's always talking about coming with me so she can check out my hot instructor. I brighten at the thought of Jake. *Maybe this is just what I need. A distraction to get my mind off Chase.*

"Hey. I'm leaving work and going to the gym now, if you want to come?" I frown when she doesn't answer. "Peyton?"

For a second, I think she's hung up on me, but then she snorts. I smile because that's just the reaction I was expecting, aside from a few missing curse words.

I'd started going to the gym nearly a month ago, after coming to an agreement with the chocolate I couldn't resist buying every weekend: I'll eat you, so long as I do my three workouts a week. I owe most of my success to Jake, my instructor. Not only because he's a great teacher, but also because he's incredibly hot. There's no better incentive than knowing you're going to be sweating it out in front of a god.

Slowly but surely, I'm starting to notice a difference. Not only in how I feel but also in how I look. I was happy with myself before, but now I'm *really* happy. And the added energy comes in handy for when Chase decides to send me out as his errand girl every five minutes. *Of course, I can think of much better ways to spend that excess energy.*

"Sorry, I was too stunned to reply. Who the hell goes to the gym on a Friday night?" Peyton finally grumbles.

"Me," I say with a grin.

"*Ohhh,*" she teases. "I get it. You're only going so you can see Fabio, aren't you? And here I was assuming that you'd developed some sort of crush on Chase."

"Of course not," I scoff, my face heating up. *Thank God she can't see me.* "And his name is Jake. I'm going there for *no* other reason than to work off some tension."

"Tension from spending the day lusting after you know who?" She snickers. "How did that go, by the way? We won't talk about how jealous I am that he took you over me. Bitch."

"It was great," I say after a moment. "From a work perspective, I learned a lot."

"And from a Chase perspective?" she pries.

"I have no idea," I admit with a sigh. "The tension that has been rising between Chase and me..."

I shake my head and swallow, my throat constricting. I'm sure I'm totally imagining that there's anything there, because I'm pretty sure he's not sitting at home thinking about me right now. I need to put him out of my mind, but that's proving really hard to do. Especially when I can't stop thinking about him.

"So, given a choice, who would you do? Hot gym instructor or Chase?" Peyton asks with a giggle.

"Considering that I have *no* chance with Chase, I'm going to say Jake," I retort.

"Wow, that's a big call."

"Did you *see* me yesterday when I totally humiliated myself?" I ask her with a frown.

Is it really such a surprise that I don't even consider Chase an option?

If I thought I had a chance with him, then things might be different. But even if he *was* interested in me, it certainly wouldn't be for anything other than a casual hook-up. That's the last thing I want with someone I have to face at work every day. Especially my boss. If I went there, then I could kiss any chance of a promotion goodbye.

Jake, on the other hand, is perfect casual hook up material...

"So, do you still cringe when you think about yesterday?" Peyton giggles, snapping me out of my thoughts. "You pretty much offered the guy head," she reminds me.

"I'll still be cringing fifty years from now," I mumble,

rubbing my forehead. "I can't imagine anything will *ever* top that as my most embarrassing moment."

"Oh, I don't know about that. The week isn't over yet." She points out. "Anyway, have fun at the gym and come over later if you like."

"Thanks, I might do that."

THE GYM IS on the other side of town from work, not far from my apartment. It's after six by the time I get there, and aside from the few other people with no social life who have also chosen to attend tonight's class, it's pretty deserted.

The class begins as usual at six fifteen, and like every other class, Jake spends half of it smiling at me. I'm standing next to the wall tonight, so there's no chance of a repeat of the barista incident.

Twice he uses me to demonstrate what he wants the class to do, which I'm sure is just an excuse to touch me. I'm fine with that, but what confuses me is the usual thrill I feel against his touch just isn't there tonight. And his smile, which usually sends my insides into a spin just isn't doing anything for me tonight.

Damn you, Chase, for getting inside my head.

When the class finishes, I take my time rolling up my mat, because I've decided that tonight is the night I make my move. After what happened with Chase, and my muddled feelings over him, I'm even more determined to do this.

I just want something to go right for once.

I want one night where I don't feel like a worthless idiot. I'm not usually the kind of girl who does one-night stands—or self-pity, for that matter—but tonight I'm willing to do whatever it takes to get Chase off my mind.

I wait until we're alone in the room before I slowly walk toward the exit. Just as I hoped, Jake jogs over to me, blocking me at the door. My heart races, because this is the biggest sign he's given me that my attraction isn't one-sided. That alone boosts my confidence.

"Hey." He grins.

"Hey," I say, trying to sound relaxed. After nearly an hour of yoga, I should be.

"You did great tonight," he comments. "I'm really noticing a difference in the way you flex."

"Thanks," I say shyly, refusing to acknowledge that his voice doesn't have me swooning like it normally would.

"So, what are you doing now?" he asks me.

I shrug. It's Friday night, and like the sad person I am, I have no plans other than to go home and watch TV in my pajamas, but I don't want him to know that.

"Nothing I can't change for the right offer," I say lightly. I'm impressed with how smooth I sound. I'm sure that has everything to do with my interest in him taking a nosedive. "Did you have something in mind?"

"I thought maybe we could go and get a drink later, or something?"

He smiles and leans a little closer to me. I swallow a shiver racing through me. Not because I like it, but because I'm feeling a little claustrophobic.

"Sure," I say. "What time?"

He glances at his phone. "I've got classes until ten, so any time after that?"

"That sounds great." I nod.

"Okay, great." He smiles. "There's a bar near my place, on the corner of Fifth and Seventh. Is eleven too late?"

"Not at all," I say, even though I'm nearly always fast asleep by then. The only thing that is worrying me is that gives me five hours to chicken out. "Eleven is perfect."

"Okay. I'll see you then." He glances at me. "I'm looking forward to it, Alana."

IT'S ONLY ONCE I'm outside the gym that the panic really begins to kick in. Whether I'm into him or not, the fact is, I haven't been on a date in months. I'm so out of practice that it will be a miracle if I can get through this without making a complete fool of myself. Considering I can't even get through a day at work without looking like an idiot, I highly doubt this is going to go smoothly.

And just like that, I'm back to thinking about Chase.

God, I wish it were him I was going out with.

My eyes widen. *Do I really think that?*

I frantically call Peyton, because she's the only one who can help me through this. Or maybe out of it. I'm not sure which yet.

"I have a date tonight and nothing to wear," I groan. "At *eleven.* Who the hell goes out that late? I'm so stupid, Pey. What the hell was I thinking, saying yes?"

"People who want to hook-up go out that late." Peyton giggles. "What are you, sixty? Who the hell goes out *before* eleven, Alana? But yay for you. This is the first step in your journey to getting yourself thoroughly fucked. So, who's the lucky guy? Hot instructor?"

"Who else would it be?" I mumble. Sex? *God, I hadn't even factored that into my anxieties until now.*

"Damn. I was kind of hoping for Chase," she admits.

So was I. I frown at myself. *Jesus, Alana, snap out of it.*

"I've only spent *one* day with him because making a fool out of myself in front of him doesn't count. Why would I be going out with him?" I say, as much to myself than her. "Actually, don't even answer that. He is the last person I want to be thinking about right now." I groan and rub my head, feeling a migraine coming on. *Isn't yoga supposed to decrease my stress levels? This is such a bad idea.*

"Stop that," Peyton says as if she can hear my thoughts. Or did I say that out loud? "Where are you meeting him?"

"Near work," I mutter hoarsely. I hunch forward, feeling sick at the thought of going through with this.

"Okay. Then come over here," she says in a no no-nonsense voice. "You'll wait with me. I've got the perfect dress you can wear. I even have some stunning new lingerie you can have. I only bought it yesterday. We can have a drink, get you nice and relaxed. We can even go over some ideas for small talk if it'll make you feel better." She pauses for a second. "Hell, we can make out if you need practice, but I draw the line at giving you head." She pauses again. "But I'm willing to consider letting *you* give *me* head."

"Maybe I should just cancel," I mumble, ignoring her attempt at humor.

"Don't you dare," Peyton protests. "You *need* this, Lanna. When was the last time you were with anyone that wasn't your hand?"

"Aaron," I admit, my voice small.

"Jesus, it's worse than I thought." She sighs.

I cringe, because I know she's right. Aaron and I broke up seven months ago, after he cheated on me with my then best friend, Dani. I'd been friends with Dani since elementary school, so it really hurt catching them in bed together.

I'll never forget walking through my apartment door after going home sick from work and finding the two of them in bed together. I heard noises that, in hindsight, were a warning, but I didn't think anything of it back then. When I pushed open the door and saw the two of them together, I felt sick. I played it back over in my mind again and again, sure that it was something I did. Did I push them together? Could I have done something differently?

But there was no indication that anything was going on between them. It was completely out of left field. It took me forever to get over it. I'm not even sure I'm completely over it now, because I'm sure it's affected my ability to trust men. I was grateful for Peyton for being there for me back then, just like I'm grateful to have her here now.

"Lanna, you *need* to do this," she says, pleading with me. "I know it's out of your comfort zone—so much so that you're probably shitting yourself, but short of hiring you an escort, I don't know what else to do with you," she says.

I laugh in spite of myself, because I know she's right. I sigh and close my eyes. *I can't believe I'm doing this.*

"Fine. I'll be there soon."

"I CAN'T DO THIS," I mumble, breaking out into a sweat.

I wipe my forehead as I pace Peyton's living room, my breathing shallow. All I think about is all the ways this can go wrong. I walk back into her bedroom and sit down on her bed. She kneels in front of me, taking my hands in hers, ready to avert my breakdown.

"Yes, you *can*," she says, staring into my eyes. "You're going to go out with Jake, have some fun, and if you end up back at his place, then you're going to fuck the cobwebs out of your vagina, okay? Do this for *you*, Lanna. Do it for your vagina."

I laugh helplessly and nod. Okay. *For me.* I nod. I *can* do this. For my vagina.

I get to my feet, feeling pumped for all of about five seconds before the sick feeling starts to creep back into my stomach. I wrap my arms around Peyton and kiss her cheek, determined to leave before I chicken out. She hands me a shot—of what, I have no idea, but I just shrug and drink it back.

"I'll call you," I promise, grabbing my purse and my phone.

She squeals and follows me to the door, hitting me on the ass as I walk out.

How did I let her talk me into this?

I should be in bed. I should be lying there, with the television on, admiring Jensen Ackles, while watching reruns of *Supernatural*, not standing in front of a bar in a dress that feels too low, too short, *and* too tight, watching Jake saunter toward me.

I brace myself as he gets closer. His dark hair blows gently against the wind. I shiver as his dark piercing eyes lock on mine and his lips part into a sexy smile.

He's much better looking than stuffy old Chase...

All I need to do now is actually believe that.

"Hey." He smiles when he reaches me. "You look incredible." He leans in to kiss me on the cheek. I nearly faint as his aftershave embraces me because it's the same one Chase wears.

"Thanks," I say, barely able to get the words out.

He takes my hand and leads me inside, wasting no time in making a move on me. We're barely through the door when his lips begin to ravage my neck. He's moving faster than I was expecting, but I go with it, because it's been that long since I've been with anyone, and Peyton is right.

I know a big part of the problem is that I'm scared to put

myself out there after what happened with Aaron, but tonight I'm going against everything my gut tells me and just going for it. *I'm going to rip it off like a Band-Aid because I'll feel so much better if I just do this.*

"Can I get you a drink?" he asks, finally dragging himself away from me long enough to look at me.

I smile. "A wine would be nice," I say. "Something white and dry."

"I'll be right back," he murmurs, stroking my arm before he steps away.

I sit down at the nearest free table and reach down to rummage through my purse for my phone. I smile when I see three messages from Peyton.

Peyton: *Everything okay?*

Peyton: *Lemme know if you need me to fake a death in the family to get you out of there.*

Peyton: *If you don't reply in five minutes, I'm coming in to save you.*

Laughing, I quickly tap out a reply to assure her I'm safe and then shove my phone back into my bag. I look around, taking in all the happy faces and laughter that fills the air. I glance back at the bar where Jake is standing, deep in conversation with the chick behind the bar. I frown as I watch her lean over a little farther, clearly trying to guide his vision to her ample cleavage. He laughs at something she says, but instead of feeling jealous, or even slightly annoyed, I feel nothing.

What the hell am I doing here? Even watching other girls checking him out isn't stirring anything inside me. It's the complete opposite reaction to watching blondie flirt with Chase earlier today. *Why can't I get him out of my head?*

"Sorry, I couldn't get away."

I look up as Jake returns to the table, carrying our drinks. He sits down and slides my wine across the table to me, his eyes burning through mine. He smiles at me just as I attempt to stifle a yawn. *Which is a great indication of how this is going.* Somehow, I manage to successfully turn it into a smirk.

"Thanks," I say, picking up my drink. I swallow a mouthful, hoping it will relax me. Or at the very least, make me feel less out of place.

"So, what do you do for work again?" he asks. He sounds genuinely interested, and I feel bad for feeling so 'meh' about this.

"I'm a junior assistant over at WPC," I say. I have to force myself to focus on him, or my attention will span elsewhere.

"Right. I think I've heard of the guy who runs that place. I'm pretty sure my sister went out with him for a bit last year. She thinks he's a bit of a cockhead," Jake says.

I giggle. *Of course, Chase went out with Jake's sister.* That's just perfect.

"He has a bit of a reputation for being difficult to get along with," I agree with a smile. "Honestly, I don't see him all that much. I'm only a junior assistant, which means I'm his *assistant's* assistant."

"The fact that his *assistant* needs help tells me either she's incredibly incompetent or he has an ego the size of Texas," he says with a laugh. "Honestly, I'm just shocked that's even a thing."

"Apparently, it is," I say. "Chase has a lot of important tasks he needs to have done, ranging from collecting his dry cleaning to fetching his coffee. They're jobs that are almost always allocated down the ranks, to me."

"Wow," Jake says, shaking his head in dismay. "So why do you work there, then? Surely there are other jobs you could get. I could put in a good word for you at the gym if you want. The reception is always looking for casual staff," he suggests.

"Thanks," I say, not wanting to point out how overqualified for that position I am. "I guess I'm just holding out hope that he sees my potential one day. My dream is to get into property analytics, and Chase's firm is one of the best property consultant firms in the country. That's the only thing that's kept me there for the last two years."

"Well, you're dedicated, I'll give you that," he says, admiration in his eyes. "Just don't let him take advantage of you."

I jump as his hand reaches out and strokes mine. He slides his finger along the back of my hand, smirking at me. I smile back, and then ease my hand away, disguising the rejection as the need for another drink. I gulp it down, emptying my glass, which he apparently finds amusing.

"Are you nervous or something?" he teases.

"Maybe slightly," I admit. *Though the alcohol certainly is helping.* "It's been a while since I've been out on a date."

I cringe at my confession. I probably shouldn't go around

admitting that, or I'll sound inexperienced and naïve. Both of which I definitely am. He flags down a waitress and orders me another drink, watching with amusement as I drink that one down too. Somewhere over the course of the evening, I begin to loosen up. That may or may not be connected to the number of drinks I consume.

For the next couple of hours, we just talk and flirt, until before I know it, it's nearly four in the morning, which is impressive, because I've never been in a bar that's open that late—not that I go to many bars. I'm pretty shocked that we found things to talk about for so long, and I'm even more shocked that I'm still awake. Other than a few sneaky strokes of my thigh under the table, he hasn't tried anything. I hate to admit it, but I've actually enjoyed myself—even if half our conversation subjects have revolved around Chase.

God, even when I'm trying to forget about him, I can't.

"I guess they're closing," Jake murmurs, glancing around.

"I guess they are," I echo with a smile. "The stacking the chairs on top of the tables *does* kind of give it away."

"Are you making fun of me?" he asks with a chuckle.

I shrug. "Maybe a little."

I stand up and groan as my head sways from the few drinks I've had. I'm relaxed and feeling great. Maybe a little too great. And frisky, which is a dangerous combination.

"So, I live not far from here," he whispers in my ear. "Want to come over for a while?" he asks, his eyes levelling on mine.

There's no questioning *why* he's asking me over; at least, not in my mind.

"Sure," I say, my heart racing.

The moment I agree, I regret it, because the nerves and doubts begin to creep in. Knowing exactly why I'm going over there is only making things worse. I'm kidding myself if I think this is anything more than me trying to get Chase out of my mind.

"Then let's go." He grins.

When we get back to his place, things quickly progress. We've barely made it through his front door, and he's undressing me. He fumbles with the zipper on the my dress, eventually tugging it free. My heart races as it slips down over my curves and pools on the floor, leaving me exposed to his intense stare.

I sigh as his fingers crawl over my bare skin. He kisses me in a way that makes me clench my thighs together. We might not have much in common, but I have no doubt that he's going to rock my world in bed.

"Come with me," he orders.

He takes my hand, slowly leading me down the narrow hallway, before hoisting me onto his hips. I gasp and wrap my arms around his neck, pressing my lips against his as his erection grinds against my thigh. *God, that feels so good already.*

"Every time I've watched you bend over in my class I've

thought about ramming my cock hard into your pussy," he murmurs, burying his face between my breasts.

I groan and throw my head back, a thrill racing through me. He's doing everything right, but for some reason, he's not doing it for me as much as I hoped he would. He slides a finger inside my bra and massages my nipple, rolling his thumb over it. With a gasp, I close my eyes and imagine myself bent over and ready for him, while he penetrates me from behind. *God, that's better.* I bite my lip, gasping as his he explores me, but in my mind, it's Chase whose fingers are sliding in and out of me. My heart races as Jake kisses my neck.

I can't do this. Even if we are both aware that this is just a one-night thing, I can't put myself through this. Not when I'm clearly thinking about someone else. I'm so frustrated with myself. Why *him* of all people? Why Chase? Why not Liam Hemsworth—who's just as unattainable, but at least I don't have to see him every day.

I'm summoning up the courage to push Jake away, and then grabbing my dress and bolting out of his apartment when I hear a noise. I frown and glance at Jake, who's frozen on the spot, a look of fear in his eyes.

"What's that?" I ask, because it sounds like someone just walked into his apartment. He's gone white. So white, I'm afraid he's about to faint on me. "Jake?" I ask, but he just stares at me, his mouth opening and closing like a fish who's struggling to breathe.

"Shit," he mutters, his eyes darting everywhere. "Fuck. *Fuck.* She's not supposed to be home for another two hours."

"Who?" I gasp, as he all but drops me on the floor.

I regain my footing, just as he grabs hold of my arm. For a second I think he's helping me catch my balance, but then I realize he's actually dragging me toward the balcony. He's got to be kidding me if he thinks I'm hiding out there. It's fucking *freezing*.

"What the hell are you doing?" I gasp as he pushes me outside. I struggle to keep the door open, but he's way too strong for me.

"Shut up, or my wife will hear you," he hisses, before slamming the door shut in my face.

His *wife*?

I turn around, my mouth still hanging open. I shake my head and laugh because it's the only thing I can do. I'm standing on the balcony of his apartment at six in the morning, freezing my fucking ass off, *in my underwear*. How the hell did this happen? How did I not pick up on the fact that he's *married*? God, I'm such a fool. Tears sting my eyes, but I wipe them away, afraid if I don't, they're going to freeze into icicles.

I need to ring Peyton.

"Shit," I curse when I remember my phone is still inside, somewhere in the living room.

If she finds my phone, my dress or looks out here, I'm dead. God, if I stay out here, I'll probably die anyway.

I glance around, trying to come up with a plan. My head is a muddle of unfinished thoughts, but I force myself to think through the haze. The fact that I'm still slightly tipsy isn't helping, and neither is the shock I'm still feeling over what has just happened.

Okay, think. There has to be a way through this.

First thing I need to do is get off this balcony. That buys me some time if she does think to look out here. I peer over the railing and shudder at how far down it is. Then I glance at the neighbor's balcony, which is almost close enough for me to touch.

Or jump over to.

Am I insane? Jumping balconies, without shoes or I don't know...clothes??

But I don't have much choice. I look at his neighbor's balcony and weigh up the pros and cons. I could slip and kill myself, but I'm confident I can make it across. The other problem is, what if his neighbor is a psycho? If I jump, I'll be stuck there, because it's the corner apartment. What if being there is a worse choice than staying here?

Besides, what exactly is my plan when I get over there? Wake them up and tell them I locked myself out? I sleepwalked onto my balcony, and the door closed behind me? They'll know right away that I'm full of shit. *So what if they do? If they let me in, the second I'm out that front door I never have to see them again.* It's one moment of shame that I'll never have to relive again.

It's either that or Jake's wife finds me.

I take a deep breath, my heart pounding. Carefully, I scale the railing and lean across, my hand almost slipping against the wet metal. My pulse hammers out of control as I ease myself over. *Don't look down.* Daylight is just starting to break through, which, considering I'm in my underwear, is not good, but I can't think about that now. One. Two. Three. My chest aches as I breathe in a lungful of cool, crisp air, and then I jump, not giving myself a chance to second-guess. I land on the platform on my side, my heart pounding.

Holy shit, I did it. I made it across.

Taking deep breaths, I try to relax, but it's hard when I'm too busy patting myself on the back. I'm pretty impressed with myself right now. I didn't know I had the strength or courage to do what I just did. Maybe I should take up base jumping.

Crawling onto my ass, I lean against the wall and peer inside the window. The light is on, so that's a good sign. All I have to do now is work up the courage to knock. *Easy. You did the hard part. Knock on the window, they'll let you in, call a cab, and you'll be home before you know it.*

I get to my feet. My whole body trembles as I work up the courage to do this. I'm almost there mentally when I decide to have one more peek inside.

Big mistake.

My eyes widen as I stare in through the living room window. *Oh god no.* Please, please not him. But there's no denying it. I'm staring directly at Chase. I'm standing on the balcony that belongs to the very man who, less than forty-eight hours ago, overheard me saying how much I want to suck his cock. *In my fucking underwear.*

I'm going to be sick.

I spin around and stand flush against the wall, gasping at

how cold the brick cladding is. I'm desperately trying to think of another solution, but there's nothing. I glance over at Jake's balcony, and see the lights are still on inside. *All she has to do is find my dress or my phone and look out here.* This is going to be a whole lot worse if I have to admit to Chase *why* I'm out here.

I look around, one more time, but there is nowhere left to go. Other than down. An eight-story fall would finish me, and huddling on the balcony in this weather would probably kill me too. I've got about ten seconds to decide what I'm going to do.

Either I scale back over and deal with Jake's wife, or I knock and deal with Chase. Hell, there isn't even a decision to *make*, because there is only one choice.

I have to knock.

I have to suck it up and knock on my boss's door, while I'm wearing nothing but my underwear. Underwear that I'm practically popping out of. *Damn Peyton and her tiny, perky breasts.* My hands shaking, I take a deep breath and bring my fist up to the door and knock.

And just when I thought I couldn't embarrass myself any harder in front of Chase.

CHAPTER SIX
CHASE

I SIT BACK in my chair and sigh as I rub my forehead. It's so late that it's almost daylight outside and my head is aching from spending way too much time staring at the same page of numbers. *I've got to get some sleep, or I'm going to drive myself insane.*

The problem is, I know the moment I close my eyes, all I'm going to be able to think about is my brother and my ex-wife.

I've been sitting here working since I got home last night. I use the term "work" loosely because I've barely made a dent in the report that I need to be finished for tomorrow's meeting. I haven't even finished balancing the expense sheets for last month, which should've been done yesterday.

Spending the afternoon being fitted for a suit for a wedding I never wanted to be a part of in the first place is what's put me in this bad mood. What I thought was going to take an hour at most, ended up eating into three hours of my time. It was late by the time I got back, and, because I was already behind after spending the day in a meeting I *really* didn't need to be at, meaning that an all-nighter was necessary. But it turns out even that wasn't going to help get this done.

Yep, I'm pretty much fucked.

Standing up, I stalk across the room to the bar and pour myself a drink and gulp it down. I don't like mixing alcohol with work because it dulls my senses, but let's face it, a drink isn't going to make the slightest bit of difference at this point. *Fuck it. I'll have another.* Maybe then, I can forget for five minutes that Josh is marrying Casey.

I told him I was okay with it, but I'm not. I'm hurt, annoyed, and I'm frustrated as fuck. The worst thing is that I have to suck all that up and plaster a smile on my face. I have to pretend I'm good with this because I know venting that to Josh will only strain our relationship even more.

The truth is, I miss my brother. I miss the way we used to be. But I'd be stupid to think after everything that's happened, we could ever go back to the way we were.

Loosening my shirt, I set my drink down and then unbutton my cuffs and my shirt. I shrug it off and then pick up my drink, wandering back over to the couch to sit down. I lean back and close my eyes, rubbing the back of my neck. I could really go for a massage right now. Especially one with a happy ending.

What the fuck was that?

My head whips sideways to the balcony. I frown because I'm sure I heard something. It could just be my mind playing tricks on me. I've been up all night, after all, and I had one hell of a day yesterday. I shake my head. That must be it. But then I hear it again. *Okay, that definitely wasn't my imagination.* Someone is trying to break in.

I snap into action mode and hurl myself off the couch, ready to take down whoever the hell has decided to mess with me while I'm in this foul mood. I thrust back the curtains and brace myself for confrontation. My eyes widen. *Okay,* now I'm *sure* that I'm imagining things. Alana Morrison, on my balcony at six in the morning, in her *underwear*?

I'm pretty sure I had this fantasy last night

Quickly recovering from my shock, I unlock the door and slide it open, a smirk spreading across my lips. I rest my hand casually against the wall as I stare at her. Maybe she's the perfect distraction. God knows she keeps throwing herself at me. Who am I to stand in the way of her dreams?

"When I told you to focus more on your work, this wasn't exactly what I had in mind," I say, not bothering to hide the amusement in my voice.

She flushes and looks down, her arms wrapping tightly around her chest.

I snort because it does nothing to cover the way she's bursting out of that bra. My cock twitches, making it clear what he's hoping for. She glares at me, obviously not enjoying that I'm finding this so funny.

Maybe she heard my prayers for a happy ending and came running?

"Can I come in?" she asks stiffly.

"Sure," I say.

Stepping back, I make sure that I'm close enough so that she has to slide her body against mine to get in. I chuckle and shake my head because this is just too fucking perfect not to make the most of it.

"Congratulations, by the way," I add.

"What do you mean?" she asks, frowning at me.

"I mean I'm used to women throwing themselves at me, but I've never had anyone try and break in through my balcony," I explain with a chuckle. "I admire your dedication."

"First of all, I am not *throwing* myself at you, and second, I wasn't breaking in," she retorts defensively. "Didn't you hear me knocking?"

She walks farther inside, and I close the door, my gaze following her across the room. My eyes are firmly on her ass as her hips gently sway which every step. My jaw tightens at the sight of her panties riding up her ass.

What the hell is she doing on my balcony in her underwear?

I'm surprised I have time to think that—considering how busy I am imagining what she would look like with those tiny panties off. I sigh, the thought my tongue sliding along her bare pussy is nearly too much for me to handle.

She sits down on my couch, carefully trying to cover herself up, much to my amusement. I walk over there and stand against the wall, knowing I'll have the best view of her there. She flushes as I stare at her.

"So, are you going to explain to me *why* you're on my balcony at six in the morning, wearing next to nothing?" I finally ask.

She glances down, her face going crimson as if I've just reminded her that she's practically naked. I step forward and lean against the back of my armchair, mainly because I'm so fucking hard it's getting uncomfortable.

"It's a long story," she mumbles.

I shrug, spreading my hands out. "I've got time."

The combination of lack of sleep, alcohol, and her turning up in her underwear is driving me crazy. Inappropriate visions pour through my mind of her crouched on her knees, wrapping those plump, red lips around my length.

She glares at me. "I really don't want to get into it right now. Do you have a shirt or something I can borrow?" she asks. She's shaking. I'm not sure if she's cold, or just really fucking embarrassed.

"Sure," I say.

I walk down to my bedroom, ramping up the heating on the way. I retrieve the lilac sweater that's been hiding in my closet for the last few months. Honestly, I've got no idea who left it here, but I knew it would come in handy one day. I walk out and toss it to her. She gratefully puts it on. I grin as it clings to her petite frame and barely covers her waist. Her eyes blaze as she glares at me.

"This is all you have? Do you even know who it belongs to?" she asks accusingly.

"Yes, and no. Sorry, it's laundry day." I smirk, even though I've got a closet full of shirts that would cover way more of her, and she knows it.

I much prefer to have this conversation with her wearing as little as possible.

Watching her sitting here in that sweater is doing nothing to tame my erection, though. At this point, I think the only fix is going to involve plunging my length into her pussy. Or down her throat, because at least I already know she's up for that.

Contrary to what most people believe, I don't wave my cock at everything that moves. Just *most* things. But there was something about Alana that sparked my interest. And when she turns up at my apartment in nothing but a skimpy set of underwear, how am I'm expected to react?

"Can I get you a coffee or something?" I ask her. She nods and even manages a smile.

"That would be good," she says.

I walk into the kitchen, glancing back to check on her every now and then. I'm dying to know what happened, but she's keeping pretty tight-lipped on the details.

"So, you haven't told me how you wound up on my balcony yet," I point out as I fill the coffee pot.

"I know," she says, her face going red. "There's a reason for that. It's embarrassing enough, without you knowing all the details. I feel sick every time I think about it."

I frown. "Is this something that I should involve the police over?" I ask.

She glares at me, her eyes flashing. "You think I'm *stalking* you?"

I chuckle at her feistiness. "That's not what I meant. I was asking if someone hurt you?"

"No, it's nothing like that," she mumbles. "Well, unless you count my dignity because that's pretty much shattered." She frowns and looks up at me. "I just don't want this to affect my position at work," she says softly.

I smirk because her only position I care about at the moment is the one that allows me to slide my cock inside her at the right angle.

"How about this," I begin. "You tell me *why* you're here, and then we can forget this ever happened."

"Really?" she asks, frowning at me like she doesn't quite believe me.

I nod, even though she's right not to trust me. I have no intention of ever letting her live this down.

"Okay. I'll tell you, but if you laugh..." I hold my hands up and put on my most innocent expression. She sighs and closes her eyes before speaking. "My gym instructor invited me out for a drink last night. I went, we got talking, and things progressed back to *his* place. I was about to leave before anything really happened, but before I got the chance, his wife interrupted us."

"His *wife*?" I say, unable to hide my grin. She nods, frowning at me. "Why wasn't he doing it for you?"

"*Pardon*?" she asks, bewildered.

"You said you were about to leave, so I assume he wasn't doing it for you. Why not?" I ask with interest.

"Is that any of your business?" she sputters, her face glowing red.

I smirk at her. "I guess not. So, let me get this straight. He kicked you out onto his balcony when his wife came home? Wow, what a gentleman," I mutter, resisting the urge to go next door and punch the shit out of the creep.

She stares at me, narrowing her eyes as if my comment was a personal attack on her.

"I'm well aware of my ability to pick terrible men, thank you," she says, through gritted teeth.

"Oh, so, this isn't the first poor relationship decision you've made, then?" I ask her.

She glowers at me like she can't believe I just asked that. Hell, I'm pretty impressed with my ability to offend her too. Maybe I should go three for three.

"Excuse me? I didn't realize that I was here to discuss my love history with you," she snaps.

"I didn't realize you were going to be here at *all*, so I guess we're even." I grin.

I stare at her for a while, enjoying watching her squirm on my couch as she struggles to think of what to say next. She clears her throat, finding the courage to look me in the eye.

"Do you mind if I use your phone to call a cab?" she asks quietly.

"You went out with someone you barely know without your phone?" I ask. I frown because I thought she was smarter than that.

She glares at me like I'm the idiot.

"Do you think I'm that stupid? Wait, don't answer that," she mutters, holding up her hand. "I took my phone, but it's still next door, along with my other things."

"So, you're just going to leave them there?" I ask, confused. I laugh because, for some reason, I find that hilarious.

"I'll buy new ones," she replies defensively.

"And a new phone too?" I ask, smirking at her.

"I'm due for an upgrade," she fires back without missing a beat. "Look, can I use your phone or not?" she asks, her frustration showing. I stand up and walk toward the door, not answering her. "Where are you going?" she asks, alarm lacing her voice.

"To get your things," I say like it's the most logical thing in the world. "I feel it's my civic duty to look out for you and to make sure his wife realizes she married a giant asshole."

Alana's eyes widen. She jumps up and stands in my way, but I easily sidestep around her.

"You can't do that," she hisses, following me to the door. I turn around, trying not to focus on the way that top is riding up over her waist. "Why not?"

"Because I'm embarrassed enough as it is without *her* knowing that I landed on *your* balcony after her *husband* kicked me out," she cries angrily.

"Put yourself in her shoes. You wouldn't want to know?" I ask her pointedly as I keep walking.

"You also apparently slept with his sister," she calls out after me when it's clear her approach isn't working.

That stops me in my tracks.

"And how would you know that?" I ask, more curious than anything else. "How did you get onto the topic of me on your hot date?"

"He asked me about my job. Is it my fault if you've slept with the whole damn city?" she retorts.

"I guess not," I murmur, raising my eyebrows. I don't bother correcting her on the number of women I've slept with. It's not nearly as many as she probably thinks.

I walk out and down the few steps to my neighbor's door and pound on it. I've never actually met this guy—or his wife—even though we've both been living here for the past twelve months. I *am* finding it kind of amusing that I've slept with his sister. I'm pretty sure I know exactly who she is too, and she wasn't that good.

I glance back to see Alana peeking around the corner. I grin at her. Irritation flashes in her eyes, which makes me chuckle. You think she'd be a little more appreciative of what I'm doing for her. The door cracks open. I whip my head back around to see his wife—unless he has more women stashed in there, which wouldn't surprise me—standing there. She frowns at me.

"Can I help you?" she asks, sounding irritated.

"I sure hope you can," I begin, running a hand through my hair. "My friend left some of her things inside your apartment, and I was hoping I could retrieve them for her."

She looks confused. "What was she doing inside my apartment, exactly?"

"Right. Maybe you should ask your husband that one," I suggest with a wink. "I'll give you a hint, though. He wasn't teaching her to *knit*."

"Are you kidding me?" she says, glaring at me.

She swings the door wide open, giving me a great look at

their apartment. I'm pleased that mine is bigger—and more tastefully furnished.

"Jake, get the fuck out here," she cries.

A man who I assume is Jake appears from the bedroom, wearing only a pair of boxer shorts. He glances at me, the color draining from his face. I smile at him and wave. If he recognizes me, then he probably knows why I'm here.

"Look, I'm not here to cause trouble. I just want Alana's things," I say to him.

"Alana?" he repeats, shaking his head as if the name means nothing to him.

I laugh. *Is he really trying to play dumb?*

"Yes," I say slowly. "The chick you had in here just before your wife came home from work—" I glance at her and wince. "Early, I presume?" she nods. I turn back to Jake and shake my head. "Really, Jake? Shoving your side piece of ass, practically naked, onto the balcony so your *wife* wouldn't find out what you'd been up to? You're lucky she didn't end up with hypothermia."

"I didn't..." He glances at his wife, his desperation oozing from his voice.

"You didn't *what*?" she screams at him.

I wince as she stalks over to him and slaps him across the face. He pleads with her to listen, which leads to the two of them fighting it out, right there in front of me. I tap my foot impatiently, waiting for one of them to remember I'm standing right there. After a few moments, I realize that's not going to happen.

I spot Alana's phone peeking out from under the coffee table, so I walk over and scoop it up, along with her dress which is balled up under a cushion on the couch.

"Lovely to meet you both," I say, walking back to the door. They both turn to stare at me in shock. "If either of you ever needs anything...sugar, coffee, marriage counseling...I'm right next door."

"There," I say, smirking at her as I walk back inside my apartment. "You can put that on if you must."

She steps into her dress, slowly sliding it up over her thighs. I watch the sweater as it rises, watching her expertly dress in front of me while revealing as little as possible. She struggles with the zip, so I motion for her to turn around so I can help her out. She jumps as my fingers touch her back—accidentally, of course.

"Sorry," I murmur. An awkward silence happens between us. "I can see why he took you home," I murmur, glancing at her in that dress. "But what I don't understand is why he let you go."

She flushes and glances down, smoothing the fabric over her curves. I reach into my pocket and pull out her phone, handing it back to her.

"Thank you," she whispers.

"You don't need to go if you don't want to," I say as she walks toward the door.

She shakes her head and looks down, an embarrassed smile on her lips.

"I think I'd better. And anyway, I've wasted enough of your

time already." She hesitates and gives me a smile. "Thank you for what you did. It means a lot to me."

I nod, clenching my hands into fists. It takes every part of me to restrain from stalking over to her, pushing her body against the door and kissing the fuck out of those luscious red lips.

"Anytime," I say. "I'll see you Monday, Alana."

I watch her disappear down the hallway, and then I close the door quietly, before sauntering back into the living room. I walk over to the balcony and stare out, hoping to get another glimpse of her. She doesn't appear, and after a while, I give up and wander down to my bedroom, taking the work I really needed to finish, with me. I frown at the documents. *I'm way too tired for this.* I toss them on the floor, where I can deal with them in the morning.

I stifle a yawn and reach for my phone, scrolling through my contacts until I reach Jade. It goes straight to voicemail, which suits me fine. I wait patiently as her welcome message plays, encouraging me to leave a message after the tone.

"Jade, it's Chase," I say, walking over to my bed. "Don't bother coming into work on Monday. You're fired."

Unbuckling my pants, I shrug them off, then I place my phone on charge and climb into bed. I smile as I close my eyes and snuggle into my pillow, because that felt fucking good.

I'd been wanting to do that for a long time.

CHAPTER SEVEN
ALANA

"ALANA," Dad says, frowning at me. I wince, because I know I've been distracted right through dinner over what's going to happen when I get to work tomorrow. "Are you okay?" he asks.

"I'm fine," I say, playing with my steak. I frown as I swirl my fork around the plate. I don't even bother pretending like I usually do, because I know there's no way he'll believe that everything's okay.

"Let me guess. It's work."

I nod, praying to God he doesn't try and pry more information out of me because that would just be the cherry on top—explaining why I was on my boss's balcony, all but naked, in the early hours of the morning. Why don't I just recap the blow job conversation while I'm at it?

I sigh, feeling awful.

No matter what I do, I can't stop thinking about it. I spent today doing everything I could to try and forget, but every time

I close my eyes, I see him leaning against the doorframe, smirking at me. And that chest. I swallow. God, why did he have to have those muscles out on display like that? Seeing him with no shirt on had me thinking things I shouldn't have been thinking. For about half a second, I found myself *hoping* he'd put the moves on me, but then reality set in, and I realized what a bad idea that would be. *Way too complicated.*

"Lanni," Dad says gently.

I snap out of my thoughts long enough for my face to flush. I know I'm the worst company today, but I can't help it. And I know I'm doing nothing to diffuse his concerns about work, either.

"I think you should seriously consider finding something else. All you seem to do is stress about that place. Surely, it can't be worth it?" Dad asks with a frown.

I cringe because, although he's right, this time it's entirely my fault. In his defense, Chase has been nothing but polite, professional, and courteous. It's *me* that's been the walking sexual harassment case.

"It's not that bad, and I'm handling it," I assure him.

"Really? You're far from coping from where I'm sitting. You've barely eaten, and you look like you haven't slept in days," he points out. "Maybe I should go down and have a word with your boss," he adds.

"Please don't do that," I say, mortified at even the thought.

Suddenly, I'm ten and back in elementary school, when my father went to talk to the principal about the two girls in the year above me who relentlessly picked on me for not having a mother. His interference made the next six months pure hell, though I'd told him that they had stopped.

I don't need him to fight my battles. I can fuck things up on my own.

"I'm fine," I say with a little more force. I just want this conversation to end already. "I promise you, if this situation gets more than I can handle, then I'll leave," I say, trying to reason with him. I reach across the table and place my hand over his, hoping there's nothing but sincerity in my eyes. I must be believable, because he relaxes and then nods.

"You know I'm just worried about you, don't you?" he asks.

"I know, but maybe I should be the one worrying about you," I tease.

"Why?"

"You're getting older. You live alone. You don't have anyone to lean on other than me," I say. "Should I go on?"

He glances down and focuses on folding his napkin into quarters. I watch him, and then it hits me. Is that what he wanted to talk to me about? To tell me that he's seeing someone?

"Why did you want to have dinner again?" I ask.

"To see how you're doing," he says dismissively.

"But you said you had something to talk to me about?" I press, not letting this go. If I'm right, then I'd be nothing but happy for him.

"It's not important," he says, his face going red. My father, blushing? Now I *know* I'm right. "We can talk about it next time."

"Okay," I say, with a smirk. "If you're sure."

He'll tell me about her when he's ready.

I'm exhausted when I get home, but I know sleep isn't going to come easily. I feel like I'm awaiting my execution and doing everything I can to avoid thinking about it. But distracting myself doesn't change the fact that the end is coming. God, I haven't felt this nervous since Tyson Mills pulled my pants down in front of the entire third grade in elementary school.

Maybe on some subconscious level, I *ask* for this kind of thing to happen to me. It can't be a coincidence the number of horrifyingly embarrassing situations I've found myself getting caught in. Maybe I need to take some responsibility and own up to that. I laugh. *So now, I think I'm sabotaging myself?* I shake my head, certain that delirium is setting in. It must be the fatigue.

By three am, I've cleaned the bathroom, my bedroom, and now I've moved on to the kitchen. It's all I can do to keep my mind distracted and off Chase Winston. Nerves eat away at my stomach, making me feel sick, and when I feel sick, I can't stand to lie down.

How am I going to face him tomorrow?

What am I going to say? He saw me in my *underwear*. How do we move past that and keep things professional? Is he going to be imagining me in my undies whenever I talk to him from now on? All I need to do is catch a glimpse of that look in his eyes, and I'll *know* what he's thinking. I shiver. *God, I wish that thought didn't turn me on as much as it does...*

SOMEWHERE BETWEEN SIX and seven I fall asleep only to wake up what feels like seconds later. I glance around and realize I'm in bed and it's my alarm I'm hearing. I try burying my head under pillows to escape the sound, but it doesn't help. I think I feel worse getting a little bit of sleep, than if I'd gotten none at all.

All I want to do is roll over and go back to sleep and pretend the last forty-eight hours never happened. It rolls around in my head on repeat, like a bad song that just won't leave me alone. I cringe, my stomach churning. I feel physically ill. *Maybe I'm coming down with something.* My heart soars. That's a reason to stay home.

I'm excited about the prospect of being sick? I'm clearly losing the plot.

Going in there and facing him today will be easier than to give this another day or two to fester in my mind. Not only that but going in there today and acting like nothing happened shows him that I don't think that this is a big deal.

My reaction decides how big this is, which means I can end this before it even begins.

MY PLAN FALLS to shit the moment I get into the cab. The

whole ride to work, I fight the urge to throw up. I can tell myself it's nothing as many times as I like; actually believing it is so much harder. When I arrive at the building, I quickly find a bathroom and hurl up what little I had for breakfast. I feel marginally better, but that only lasts until I remember I'm going to have to face him today. I wash my hands, staring at my reflection in the mirror.

How on earth do I get through this?

He's going to love this. He will milk this for all it's worth, and I'll have to sit there and take it. I know he agreed he wouldn't mention it again if I told him what happened, but even *I* wasn't stupid enough to believe that. The only way he's going to let this slide is if he believes that his teasing isn't having any effect on me, and I'm not sure I can do that. How can I fool someone who gets off on toying with other people's emotions?

Because I don't have a choice.

Nodding, I take a deep breath and straighten up my shoulders.

If he thinks I'm walking in there, embarrassed and unable to look him in the eye, he's got another thing coming.

THE FIRST THING I notice when I walk into the office is that Jade's desk is empty.

The one thing I know about her is that she's always early. Like *obsessively* so. I've always tried my best to get to work ten minutes early, and she was always already there, looking like she'd been there for hours. She was the first to arrive and the last to leave. I used to joke that it was no coincidence. She lived there because it was cheaper than paying city rent.

"Is she sick?" Peyton asks, her expression perplexed.

"I don't know," I shrug. "But she's late if she *is* coming in."

"Very late for her." She gives it a moment of thought and then shakes her head. "So, anyway, why didn't you call me back?" she asks, as if just remembering she had something to be annoyed at me about.

"I was meaning to, but then I had dinner with Dad and I totally forgot," I say, making a face. She nods, completely trusting that I'm being truthful with her. I mean, why would I lie?

Because I feel foolish enough about the whole thing, without having to put what happened into words to explain it to her.

"So, am I getting the details or not?" she teases. "Did you and Jake...." She giggles and does a little dance. Then she stops, her eyes widening. She's not looking at me, though. I turn around, following her gaze. Chase stands by the door, smirking at me.

"Yes, Alana, tell me too. Did you and Jake...?" he asks, mimicking Peyton's tone. If I wasn't so horrified, I'd be laughing because he does a pretty good impression of her. "Can I please see you in my office, Alana. That is, if you can spare the time," he adds pointedly.

I flush and get to my feet and follow him over to his office. *Remember: Confidence. Eye contact. Own it.* Pfft. Easy. I breathe out as he motions for me to enter first. I do, and he follows, closing the door behind him.

He smirks as I sit down. My heart races. He promised that he wouldn't make me relive the humiliation that I was already putting myself through every day, anyway. But why else would I be in here, if not for him to rub it in? Is this what it's going to be like? Him finding excuses to get me alone and tease me? He grins at me, and behind that smirk I know exactly what he's thinking.

"I trust your day is going better than Saturday?" he asks me.

I glower at him, my anger starting to boil. He's enjoying this *way* too much.

"I thought we had an agreement to forget about that, if I told you what happened," I say, keeping my voice cool.

"We did," he nods, "but I decided to change that agreement."

"I guess that doesn't surprise me," I mutter. He raises his eyebrows, daring me to say more. *If I'm going down, I'm going down, saying what I like.* "I mean, you're not exactly known for keeping your word."

"Is that so?" he finally says. His eyes twinkle, but my confidence has caught him off guard. "Enlighten me, Alana. When have I ever gone back on my word as far as you're concerned?"

"I didn't mean *me*," I say, forcing myself to keep eye contact. "I meant, I've heard things about *you*." *Oh God, someone please stop me talking.* "But the point is, you're proving those rumors to be right. It doesn't matter if I can't back it up if you're going back on what you promised me on Saturday, does it?"

He sighs and shakes his head. He frowns, but his eyes are amused. It's like he's getting off on the fact that I'm standing up for myself. Maybe he's just in shock. Hell, I'm in shock. I never thought I had it in me.

"Fine. I won't mention it again," he says. "I'm sure it won't be long before you give me something else to tease you about," he murmurs. I glare at him, but of course, he's probably right.

"If we can get to the reason I called you in," he says, sounding official.

I swallow, my throat dry as my face heats up. *He called me in here for a legitimate reason?* I wish I'd known that five minutes ago.

"I was thinking about what I walked in on the other day. It sounded like you weren't happy with the duties you've been given as a junior assistant."

"I just think I'm more capable," I reply.

He grins "You've definitely proven yourself to be *very* capable."

I glare at him, not liking what he's insinuating.

"Is there a point to this?" I asked him.

"Yes." He coughs, clearing his throat. "My point is this. Jade has informed me that she has left, so I'll be looking for a new executive assistant. I'd like to give you a trial run. Two weeks to prove that you can handle the role. If you're successful with that, the job is yours, complete with a healthy raise." He pauses and smirks at me. "In *salary*, that is."

I stare at him, in shock. His attempt at embarrassing me goes completely over my head because I haven't gotten over the first part of what he said.

"You called me in here to *promote* me?"

He shrugs and leans back in his chair. "I called you in here to give you the *chance* at a promotion," he corrects. "So, are you going to take it, or will I be advertising this position publicly?"

I know this is probably a battle that I don't want to be fighting, but the idea of moving up and being recognized for what I can do is too tempting to ignore.

"Can I think about it?" I ask.

He looks surprised. "Sure. You have until the end of the week to let me know your decision. Does your hesitation have anything to do with your little sidekick out there?"

Shit. I hadn't even thought about Peyton.

"Not at all. If I decide to accept, I'm sure she'll be happy for me," I say, hoping that's the truth.

I WALK out of Chase's office in a state of shock. That didn't go down anything like I'd been expecting. I glance over at Jade's desk and frown. Something doesn't sit right. I don't buy his story for a second. She hadn't given any indication at all to suggest that she was thinking about leaving.

Then again, I'm probably the last person she'd tell.

The other part of me is wondering exactly what this promotion will entail. I'm opening myself up to God knows what. I really want to prove that I can handle this, but how do I know he's going to play fair? And is it a coincidence that all this is occurring after what happened on the weekend? I have so many unanswered questions.

The rest of the day I work quietly by myself, avoiding nearly every attempt that Peyton makes to engage me. If we start talking, I'll tell her, and I don't want to do that until I know what I want to do. If I can't even tell her that I've been promoted or why, then how do I expect to handle working directly for Chase? *Is advancing my career worth it, if it's at the expense of my only real friend?*

I'm beginning to think it's all more trouble than it's worth.

I RUSH out of the office as soon as work finishes to avoid talking to Peyton, but she corners me in the elevator.

"Want to come to my place for a drink?" she asks.

I take one look at the hopeful expression on her face and cave.

"Sure."

I MAKE the short walk with Peyton to her place, neither of us saying much the whole time. Once we're inside her apartment, I prepare myself for the conversation I know we need to have. She pours each of us a glass of wine and turns on some music, dancing her way over to me.

"I want to talk to you about something," I say, my heart racing. I need to get this over with before I chicken out.

"Oh? About why you've been acting super weird all day, I hope?" she asks, smirking at me.

"Sort of," I mutter. I hesitate, the sudden urge to confess everything overwhelming me. "Chase offered me a promotion," I blurt out.

"What? Wow," she mumbles, forcing herself to smile. "That's great. Congratulations. Did it have anything to do with last Thursday and what he overheard in the office?"

"I can't believe you'd even think that," I frown.

"Relax, I'm teasing you, Lanna."

Even though she's laughing, I'm not sure I believe her. She sits down and lets out a sigh, giving up her game. Her shoulders roll forward, telling me how defeated my news has made her feel.

"I'm sorry. I totally didn't mean that," she says. "If it's going to be anyone, I'm glad it's you."

"But?" I prompt her.

"It's just that Jade's job is pretty much how far I can go with the qualifications I have. But you? This is just a stepping stone for you. You'll do it for maybe a year, then you'll be somewhere else entirely, and he'll probably replace you with someone outside the office." She shakes her head sadly. "I try so hard to not let this kind of stuff get me down, but I've been working really hard. It would've been nice if he noticed or acknowledged that sometime, you know?"

I nod, feeling terrible. I've been so self-involved that I didn't even think about it like that. Sure, my qualifications outweigh hers by a mile, but she has something for this position that I'll never have—loyalty.

"Anyway," she says, wrapping her arms around me, "let's move on. Okay?"

"No," I say, not wanting to leave things like that. "Look, this has nothing to do with how hard you work or who deserves it more. *Trust* me."

"What do you mean?" she asks, confused.

I sigh and sit down, gulping down my wine. The only way for her to understand this has nothing to do with her is to tell her the whole sad and sorry story.

"You know how I went out the other night with Jake?" I say, my voice small.

"And didn't call me right away," she accuses. "Too busy getting down and dirty, huh?" She reaches over and slaps me on the arm, a big grin on her face.

"Sorry about that, and no. You'll understand in a moment," I add, when she goes to speak. "So, we ended up back at his place, only before anything really happened, his wife came home."

"His *wife*? Dude, you didn't tell me he was *married*," she hisses, her eyes wide with horror.

"I didn't know," I retort. "If I *had* known, you know I'd never have gone out with him in the first place. Anyway, that isn't the point. He pushed me out onto his balcony—in my underwear—and locked me outside."

"Fucking asshole," she rages, her dark eyes flashing.

"Oh, it gets even worse," I say in a grim voice. "I jumped

one apartment over, because I figured if anyone was going to catch me, I was better off with it being a complete stranger, rather than his wife. Right?"

"Totally," Peyton agrees. "So, what happened? You knocked on some rando's window?"

"That was my plan." I cringe, just thinking about it. "But that *rando* turned out to be Chase Winston. So, there I was, on his balcony. In my underwear. In the rain. At six in the fucking morning," I say.

She stares at me in shock and then laughs. "You knocked on our *boss's* window, in your *underwear*?" she gasps, between fits of laughter. Her eyes are so wide she looks almost comical. "Oh, Lanna! What did he do?"

"He let me in," I say. I shudder, remembering the moment he realized it was me. "He was so amused by the whole thing, and I think he loved the fact that I was so embarrassed. I asked for a shirt to cover myself up, and he gave me something that wouldn't fit even *you*," I say, eyeing her tiny, petite frame enviously.

"And now you think that's what this promotion is all about?" she asks, confused. "Because you turned up on his balcony in your underwear?"

"I'm *sure* of it. Between that and last week, he probably thinks I'm an easy score." I frown. *God knows what this promotion entails.* Between the blow job talk and the free peep show, he's probably wondering what he can get if he pays me more.

"If you really believe that, then why not just say no?" she asks. Her eyes narrow. A smile creeps across her face as she reaches over and slaps my leg again. "Ah, I get it. It's because you *like* the idea of him wanting you like that, don't you?"

I open my mouth, ready to argue, and then close it.

"Fine, maybe I do, but that doesn't mean I'm going to set myself up for disappointment," I argue.

"What do you mean? Are you worried about him hurting you?" she asks.

I snort. "God no. I *know* the type of guy he is. That part is fine. I'm scared that I'll get my hopes up about this promotion leading somewhere, when he has no intention of letting that happen."

"So, talk to him about it. If he's so sure you're an easy lay, he'll probably agree to whatever terms you throw at him."

I think about that for a second. *Maybe she's right.* Maybe I can bargain with him. I just want the chance to prove to him that I can be an asset to him in a business sense and not just run around him in circles, like a lapdog. I glance at Peyton, feeling bad for describing the job like that.

"You really think I can do that?" I ask her, hesitating.

She nods encouragingly. "Just keep your head above water and remember why *you're* doing this. You'll be fine, as long as you don't get caught up in his charms," she assures me.

"I can assure you I have *no* intention of letting him get under my skin," I say with a laugh. "I mean, sure he's attractive, rich, and he has the ability to make me feel like I'm standing in front of him, naked—"

"Because you know, that's what you're known for now," Peyton cuts in with a giggle. I glower at her and then continue.

"As I was *saying*, I can think of a thousand other gorgeous guys I could be with who'd be much less trouble." I say. Peyton raises her eyebrows, as if she doesn't quite believe me.

Hell, I'm not sure I even believe it myself.

The biggest problem is that I don't know if I can be that close to him every *single* day and not give in if he made a move on me. *And here I go again, thinking that he's even interested in me like that.* I bet this is nothing more than a game for him. I'm just another chick throwing myself at him, only I'm more creative about it than most. He probably fired Jade, just so we could mess with my head some more.

"Still not convinced?" Peyton asks.

"I'm just not sure that it's worth losing my sanity over," I say honestly.

"What do you mean? It's a great opportunity for you. Isn't this why you're still here? Hoping for a chance like this to pop up?"

"But that's just it," I argue. "This isn't a chance to further my career. He doesn't see potential in me. He sees a chance of getting himself some action. I'm sure that's all this is. His way of trying to work his way between my legs."

"What you're describing wouldn't really be that bad," Peyton smirks. I roll my eyes.

"You know what I mean," I say. "I don't want to get my hopes up and think this could actually go somewhere for my career and then have it fizzle into nothing."

"But you don't know until you try. If you're right, and this is all just to get you into bed, then you can sue him for sexual harassment and make millions anyway," she says with a sly grin.

I chuckle because I know she's only *half* joking.

"I guess I don't have much to lose," I say slowly.

She's right. I can look at this however I want to. As an opportunity to further my career, with the added bonus of getting closer to Chase, or I can psych myself out so much that I decline his offer.

"Okay," I say, my heart pounding. "I'll do it."

"Good," Peyton says with a nod. "Now, where's your phone?"

"Why?" I ask, confused.

"Because now that you've made up your mind, you're calling him before you change it again."

I scowl at her, and she grins back at me. "I know you, Alana. You'll have talked yourself out of this by morning if you don't set it in stone now. Am I wrong?"

"Okay," I grumble, poking my tongue out at her.

Maybe there's some truth to what she's saying. I grab my phone. My hands shake as I dial his number. I'm praying that he doesn't answer, but, of course, he does.

"Hello," his smooth voice comes down the line.

My heart thumps. I think about hanging up, but instead, I swallow my anxieties and force myself to speak.

"Fine. I'll do it."

"Well, that's great," he says. "They're my favorite words to hear from a woman. Now, would you mind being more specific, starting with who you are?" I open my mouth, not sure how to respond to that. “Relax, Alana. I’m joking,” he chuckles.

Asshole.

“I’ll see you tomorrow,” I say stiffly.

“No, you’ll see me tonight, actually,” he replies. “I need you to go to my office and grab the Fletcher files for me and deliver them to my apartment. You remember where I live, right?”

“You know damn well I do,” I growl, my face heating.

“Good, then I’ll let the doorman know you’ll be in. I’ll see you soon.”

He hangs up. I stare at my phone, in shock over what just happened. How did I agree to that? Is that what this is going to be like—being on call at all hours?

The plan was to call him and set this thing in stone, so I’d have the weekend to get used to the idea of working so closely to him. I certainly wasn’t expecting him to put me to work now.

“How did it go?” Peyton asks impatiently.

“I’m, uh, I’m going over to his place.” I swallow, my throat as rough as sandpaper. “Now.”

“Now?” she cries.

“He wants me to collect a file from his office and deliver it to him,” I explain.

“Then tell him to call an Uber,” Peyton retorts, waving her hand. “Surely, he can’t expect you to be on call twenty-four-seven, can he?” she asks. “You’re going over there and you’re going to set some boundaries. He’s seeing how far he can bend you.” She narrows her eyes when I flush. “*Figuratively* speaking, Alana.”

"So, what do I do?" I ask helplessly.

She smiles. "Use this to your advantage."

"What do you mean?" I say. I have no idea how to do that.

"He wants you to work for him, and he's testing your boundaries, so test his right back. Push his limits. Ask for more money or an even bigger promotion. Forget an internship. Ask him to hire you as a permanent junior analyst."

"But that's the thing. He has a team who have been there for years. He doesn't even hire junior analysts. Only people who have years and years of experience," I say with a frown. An internship is my best way to get into something that even comes close to matching my qualifications.

"So? The worst he'll say is no, so then you say okay, give me an internship. But imagine if he agreed?" she says. "You'd be *in*, Lanna."

My heart races as I think about what she's suggesting.

There's no way he'd agree to that...would he?

CHAPTER EIGHT
CHASE

I REALLY DID NEED the files.

Sure, I could've gone over there myself to get them or called a twenty-four-hour courier service, but it's so much more fun making her do it. That and she probably thinks that this is all just a game to get her into bed. Maybe a part of me *does* want that, but this is also about recognizing when one of my staff is unhappy and seeing how far they'll go to get what they want.

I pour myself a drink and wait for her to arrive with the files. I'm impressed when it takes her less than half an hour to get from her place to the office and then to my apartment. I'm standing at the door, leaning against the frame when she exits the lift. She flushes when she sees me. I smirk back. She doesn't need to know I've been standing like this, waiting, for the last ten minutes.

"Sorry, I wasn't sure if you wanted to use the door or the balcony again," I tease her. She scowls at me and steps forward, pressing the file firmly against my chest. Then, she steps back to examine me. "Thanks," I say. I saunter back inside and over to the kitchen, tossing the files onto the counter. "It turns out I didn't need them so urgently, after all."

"Why doesn't that shock me," she mutters. She shakes her head, looking like she's about to say something, but then reconsiders, biting back her words.

"Since you're here," I motion for her to come inside. "How about we discuss the terms of your promotion now?"

"That sounds great, actually," she says. I raise my eyebrows as she walks inside, closing the door behind her. She takes a seat on my couch, while I watch her thoughtfully. "Because I have a few conditions of my own that I would like to bring up."

I don't bother trying to hide my amusement. Instead I just straight out chuckle, which seems to infuriate her.

"Drink?" I ask her.

She shakes her head. "I wouldn't want to make this feel like anything other than a business meeting," she replies evenly.

"Why else would you be at my apartment after hours, if not for business?" I murmur. She flushes at that comment. "So," I continue, "you mentioned you had conditions?"

"I want you to hire me as a junior analyst."

I stare at her, admiring her confidence, and then I shrug.

"Sorry. I don't do them."

"So, make an exception."

"I'm not letting you pick and choose your position at my company, Alana," I say, frowning. "I'm offering you an executive assistant position."

"Which you must realize isn't something I'm interested in doing for you, long term," I argue.

"I'm not sure if you *understand* how this boss slash employee thing works, but you probably shouldn't alert me to the fact that you're not loyal to your position," I reply. I'm trying to keep the amusement out of my voice, but it's hard.

"I've been working for you for two years. I've showed my loyalty," she says. *She's standing her ground.* I like that. A lot. "I'm being honest with you about what I want out of this."

I sigh. "Okay. How about this? You prove to me you can handle being my assistant for a month, and I'll consider allowing you to join the analytics department—on an internship."

"Consider?" she repeats, raising her eyebrows.

I chuckle. "Fine. I'll *offer* you an internship."

She hesitates. "I also want to be clear about something else. I'm not here to be your new toy. I'll do whatever you ask me to, but if you step over the line, I'm done."

"And what exactly would constitute that?" I ask calmly. "Me arriving on your doorstep in my underwear? Or maybe announcing to the office how badly I want to lick your pussy?"

Her eyes widen, and her mouth falls open. I smile, because that was exactly the reaction I was going for. She quickly recovers and presses her lips together. She glowers at me, before standing and stalking to the door.

"I'll see you tomorrow, Mr. Winston," she says, her voice stiff.

"I'm looking forward to it," I grin.

I WATCH her disappear down the hallway, my eyes focused firmly on her ass. I'm so distracted that I don't hear the sound of my phone ringing at first. It stops by the time I race over to answer it. I frown when I see Josh's name and call him back.

"Sorry, I was busy." I shut the door and wander into the kitchen and pour myself a drink. "What's up?"

"Can I drop past? I'm literally outside your place right now."

"Yeah, sure," I say, not sure what he wants, especially so late in the evening. "Come on up."

I end the call and walk over to the living room window, where I can see him disappearing into the lobby. I wait a few minutes and then walk to the door. I open it, just as he appears from the elevator.

"Can I get you a drink?" I ask him as he walks inside.

He shakes his head as I close the door behind him.

"I can't stay. I'm meeting..." His voice trails off. He doesn't need to say it. He's meeting his fiancée.

My ex-wife.

"What did you want to talk to me about, then?" I ask.

"I just wanted to check in and make sure that you're still okay with coming to the wedding? It's kind of getting close, so we're confirming all the details." He pauses for a moment. "Will you, uh, be bringing anyone along?"

"Yes," I respond, taking a mouthful of drink. Is that why he's here? To scope out whether I'm coming alone or with a date? Which would he consider worse? He waits patiently for me to elaborate, but I don't.

"Are you seeing someone, then?" he asks.

I nod. "You'll love her. Maybe if things with Casey don't work out, you can steal her from me too?" Josh frowns at me. I flash him a smile. "I'm kidding."

"Not funny," he retorts. "I forgot how messed up your sense of humor can be. If you're *really* seeing someone, she must be pretty special to put up with your shit. I can't wait to meet her." He glances at his watch and makes a face. "I have to go."

"Okay. Thanks for stopping by," I say, still not entirely sure what the reasoning behind his visit is. I follow him to the door. He turns around.

"What did you say your girlfriend's name was? For the seating arrangements," he quickly adds.

"Her name?" I repeat. He nods.

"Alana," I say calmly.

CHAPTER NINE
ALANA

I SIT at my kitchen table and gulp down the last of my coffee, then I stand up and put the cup in the dishwasher. I'm feeling buzzed, but I'm pretty sure that's just because I've had my daily caffeine limit in the last two hours alone. I've been up since five, because I was too nervous and excited to sleep. Things are finally starting to happen and it's only taken me two years to get there. This time in two short weeks, I'll be working in the analytics department.

I just have to get through working for Chase first.

The job itself doesn't make me nervous, but Chase sure as hell does. Sometimes I wish I could just flip everything up on itself and be the one that's in control. He intimidates me so much that I just don't know how to make that happen. I hate how he can completely mess up my entire train thought just by flashing one of his smiles. The thought of working closely with him is mildly terrifying.

I probably won't even be around him that much. At least, that's what I'm telling myself. My office is far enough away from his that I'll be able to escape when I need to. The reality is, things aren't going to be much different than they were before. I'll even still get to see Peyton every day. The only difference is that I'll technically be her boss.

By the time I arrive at the office, my nerves have all but disappeared—until I walk into my office and see my desk isn't there. I frown and turn around. Peyton, who is already at her desk smiles weakly at me.

"They moved it out about ten minutes ago," she explains. "I guess he decided to shake things up a bit?"

I nod grimly. "I guess he did."

I give her a quick smile and then march across the hall to Chase's office.

Sure enough, when I walk in, there my desk, with my things packed neatly in a box next to it. The thing about Chase's office is that it was originally designed to be just like it is now, with his assistant right outside. I've never seen it set up that way, though. It's always been Jade, in with us and this room set up as a waiting area, complete with an oversized couch and a coffee table. The couch and coffee table are gone, replaced with two modest chairs and a small plant. Chase walks out of his office, smirking when he sees me.

"Alana. I assumed that you wouldn't mind if I changed things up a little," he says, almost daring me to question his authority. "I figured that my assistant should have her own space, away from those she's supposed to be in charge of," he adds.

Like Jade did?

"Of course, it's fine. It makes sense," I say, forcing myself to smile.

He nods. "Good. I'll be in my office if you need anything."

He disappears back into his office, leaving me alone to gather my thoughts. Sitting down, I take a deep breath. This isn't such a big deal. If anything, it's a good way to ease myself into things changing. *Two weeks. I just need to push through and do this for two weeks.*

I'm all psyched up to start my work, but when I glance at my empty desk, I realize that I have no idea what I need to get done. Even though Jade worked in the same room as me, I never really paid much attention to what she did. Probably because I spent all my time trying to forget she was there. Hell, I don't even know how this intercom works.

I give it a few minutes before I walk over to his door and knock.

"Yes?" he calls out. He looks up at smiles at me as I walk in. "Struggling with something already?"

I frown at him. "I just want to know what you'd like me to do," I say in what I hope is a friendly voice.

"I didn't think you'd need that much direction," he muses. He leans back in his chair and studies me. "I mean, it's not like you didn't work in the same *room* as my last assistant for two years. Too busy polishing your nails to notice anything that she was doing?"

"Too busy fetching your coffee you mean," I respond, my voice frosty. I take a deep breath to calm myself down and then I try a different approach. "Look, I need you to understand that this is my first day in a new role and tell me what you expect of me," I say firmly. "This will be painful for the both of us if you don't meet me halfway." *I'm holding my ground and it feels good.*

He stares at me for a moment and then nods.

"I need my meetings booked for next week. I need my dictation typed up and emailed to me so that I can open it on my computer." He stands up and walks over to the filing cabinet near the window, retrieving a stack of folders on top of it. "And I need to go through these and pick one that stands out for you."

"What are these?" I ask, grunting as he tosses the folders into my arms. "Proposals. They're companies that are close to going under."

"Okay," I say.

A surge of excitement hits me. *I don't remember Jade doing this kind of thing.* He picks up his phone and looks at me, as if wondering why I'm still here. I flush and walk over to the door, struggling to close it after me. He looks up at me and smiles.

"Oh, Alana?" he says.

"Yes?" I ask, looking up at him.

"There is a job description in the top drawer of your desk,

complete with a detailed list of what I expect from you on a daily basis," he says, his eyes locking on mine.

I glare at him. *Why the hell didn't he just tell me that in the first place?*

"Thanks," I say stiffly as I close the door with a thud.

I'm still fuming when I sit back down at my desk. I pull out the description, almost scared to see what it entails, but as I read through it, my nerves subside. Everything on his list I'm confident I can handle. *Oh well. At least I have a plan now.*

I DON'T SEE Chase for the rest of the day, because he's out of one meeting and into the next. The few times I *do* see him, he still manages to make me feel flustered and nervous, even though he's being nothing but professional.

BY THE END of the day I'm exhausted and glad to be going home. Maybe it's just the fact that I've been awake since five this morning, but I don't remember being this tired when I was just a junior assistant. I walk outside the building, nearly colliding with Peyton as I walk round the corner. She smiles at me.

"Finally," she says. "I've been waiting for you. How did it go?" she asks impatiently.

"It was fine, I guess," I say, shrugging.

"Just fine? Did he fuck you on his desk?" she giggles.

"No. He was completely professional," I say, making a face.

"I enjoyed it, but I think it's going to take me a few days to get used to the change. Want to go and get a coffee or something?" I ask her.

She shakes her head, her eyes sparkling. "I would, but I have a date."

"Ooh, lucky you," I grin. "Who is he?"

"Just a guy I've been talking to. My cousin gave him my number and we've been chatting on the phone and online. He's a vet. He has three dogs."

I giggle. "You're allergic to dogs."

She waves her hand dismissively. "Minor complication."

"Well, have fun and call me with the details," I say.

I give her a hug and then walk across the road to flag down a cab, secretly glad she's busy tonight. All I want to do is go home and relax.

Even though my thoughts are all over the place and I'm still adjusting to the changes at work, I'm pretty proud of myself. So much has happened in the last week, and while it hasn't all been good, I'm at least putting self out there and trying new things. Instead of hiding in my shell, I'm pushing myself for once and standing up for what I want. I'm taking risks and some of them are even paying off.

It's nearing the end of my first week, and working directly for Chase is nothing like I thought it would be. He's been nothing but professional and courteous the entire time.

To top it off, I'm really enjoying the extra responsibilities that come with my new arrangement. The only bad thing about this new role is that I don't get to see Peyton nearly as much and I'm worried it's going to change our relationship.

As I walk over to my old office to collect a file from Peyton, I stop at the door and listen to the sound of giggling and laughter coming from inside. My new replacement started yesterday, and it seems she and Peyton get on just great. I wish I didn't feel jealous, but I do. I can't help but feel like while I'm moving up on the career ladder, I'm going to be losing my best friend in the process.

Taking a deep breath, I push open the door and walk in. Just like that, whispers stop. I stare at Peyton and then at the new girl. Both of them are sitting at their desks, heads down, engrossed in their work. I frown and march over to Peyton, mumbling something about the Christenson file. She smiles and hands it to me, then goes back to her work. I wait for a second, before I turn around and walk out, pretending that I don't care, even though I do. I'm hurt and blinking back tears. I've never seen Peyton that into her work in the two years I've known her.

Am I the new Jade. Is that what this is?

I sit back down at my desk, not sure what to do. Maybe I'm imagining it, but what if I'm not? I never considered that we were only friends because we worked together. It never entered my mind that our relationship would change if we no longer had that connection in common. *I hate the thought of losing my best friend.*

I force myself to focus on my work and forget about Peyton. It's hard to concentrate at first, but by the time lunch rolls around, I'm in my groove. I'm halfway through my current task and feeling much more optimistic, so I push that aside and reach for the stack of proposals he wants me to go through. He's not expecting this until next week, but I'm determined to get it done early. Yes, I'm trying to impress him, but it has nothing to do with wanting him to like me. I just want him to appreciate what I can do.

Chase walks out of his office and over to me, resting his hands on the edge of my desk, so he's facing me. I tense, because no matter what I do, I can't seem to shake the attraction I have for him.

"I just thought I'd check in on how you're doing?" he says.

He's almost close enough for me to kiss. I study his lips for a moment, wondering how they'd feel, pressed up against mine. *Would he be rough? Or gentle?*

"Alana?"

I blush as he jolts me out of my daydream and stare at him. I scold myself for even letting my mind wander there, while he raises his eyebrows, waiting for an answer.

Shit.

"Sorry," I say, my tone way too upbeat. "I guess I was so into my work that I didn't even hear you coming."

"Funny," he grins. "Most women complain I'm too loud." I flush at his joke, cursing myself for my choice of words. "And I'm glad to hear things are going well." He glances at his watch.

"Although, you do realize that you're five minutes into your lunch break already?"

I nod and hold up a soggy cheese and tomato sandwich that looks anything but appetizing.

"I brought a lunch from home," I explain, embarrassed. "Who knew that tomato makes bread go soggy? Anyway, it doesn't matter. I was going to get a head start on that dictation you wanted typed up, anyway."

He chuckles and reaches into his back pocket to pull out his wallet. He flicks it open and hands me his credit card.

"Go over to Watson's and get me a sandwich. They know me, and they know what I like. Order one for yourself, too," he says. I shrug and stand up, my stomach demanding that I accept his kind offer. "And please don't work through lunch again, Alana. I don't want you to sacrifice your own time for me," he says with a frown.

I stare at him with raised eyebrows.

"Then why did you have me drop a file off to you at ten o'clock at night?" I ask sweetly. I smirk at him and walk out the door before he can answer.

I USE the short walk over there to catch up on my personal emails—not that I have many to go through. The one that stands out is from my father. It instantly makes me frown, because he's so technologically challenged. I click on it, expecting it to be spam, but I'm impressed when I realize that it *is* from him.

Hey Lanni I hope you're okay I was worried when you didn't turn up I tried calling but I couldn't get through to you how about dinner next week maybe Friday? Dad

Shit.

I'd totally forgotten about dinner. I glance at the email again and burst out laughing. Not only does my father apparently not understand the importance of grammar, but he sent the email to every single person in his contact list.

I'm still chuckling as I tap out a reply.

Hey Dad,

Friday sounds good, but you'd better book a big table, considering you invited fifty-seven people. Sorry about missing dinner; I completely forgot about it. See you soon.

Love Lanni.

I shove my phone back in my pocket just as I reach the café. I walk inside, pleased to see that it's quieter than I was expecting it to be. I wander up to the counter and order without having to wait.

As I wait for my order, I stifle a yawn. I'm so tired. The late nights and early mornings are really starting to mess with my head, but I'm determined to do whatever I have to, in order to impress Chase, because I'm getting this internship, one way or another. *I hoped I'd be getting more than just a promotion,*

God, I confuse myself sometimes. One minute, I'm upset because I think he's only promoting me for sex, and the next, I'm upset because nothing has happened. I had this idea in my head about us working closely together, side by side, with the sexual tension rising by the second. He'd look at me and my heart would race, and then he'd lean in and kiss me.

But that just isn't how it's happening, and I'm embarrassed to admit that I'm disappointed. *Do I like him? God, I think I do.* I think the disappointment that I'm feeling is because I'm worried that maybe he's not that attracted to me after all.

By the time I get back to the office and give Chase his lunch, I'm feeling very deflated. I sit at my desk, picking at my sandwich while I get back to working on the proposals. I'm not certain, but I think this is just a test. I don't think he is considering any of these companies for a takeover bid. Either way, I'm determined to show him that I can handle this.

When I block out every other thought and force myself to focus only on what I'm working on, the time seems to fly. I've picked out my top choice, so now I'm just gathering the statistics to back up my decision.

"Alana?"

I look up and see Chase staring at me.

"I just asked you if you're planning on going home tonight or not," he repeats in a mocking tone. "It's after six," he adds.

I glance down at the stack of work in front of me and frown. I hate the idea of not getting this finished almost as much as I hate the idea of having a boss who won't let me work overtime.

"What are you working on?" he asks, wandering over.

"You asked me to look over those proposals," I say. "And I've done that."

I hold up the file containing the company I consider the best gamble. He outstretches his hand and takes it from me, then he looks back at me.

"And this is what you've chosen as my next investment?" he asks with interest.

"Yes," I say, anxious to hear his response.

I know it's not the most obvious choice, but I put a lot of consideration into choosing it. He nods and then glances at his watch.

"Would you mind running through this with me now? I know I said that I didn't want you working into your own time, so I'll pay you, of course."

I nod. "Sure."

We walk into his office. I sit down, my body tensing when he sits next to me, rather than behind his desk. I'm nervous that I'm about to make a fool of myself. He might hate my ideas. I thrust my handwritten notes in his face. He takes them from me and reads through them, his expression thoughtful.

"I thought Benson had the least potential for growth," he frowns, examining the file. "It makes it a really hard sell when the buyer can't see their investment paying off within a specific time frame," he explains, glancing at me.

"I know. I was thinking the same, until I saw this," I hand him another report. "These are the figures for the last twelve months for what is pretty much an identical product on the market, made by a competitor. The only difference is their product doesn't do half the things that the other one can."

"So what you're saying is that even though they don't look like much of a threat right now, with the right marketing and the right match..."

His voice trails off as he looks at me. I nod, unable to contain my excitement.

"This is good," he says. He nods slowly and then glances at me, the look in his eyes driving me crazy. I love impressing him almost as much as I love the thought of pleasing him. "But, it's still a big risk."

"With a big reward," I argue. "Over a safer option that will net a buyer a much smaller return."

"You've put a lot of work into this," he murmurs. "I'm impressed you've done all of this in just a few hours. Still, I'm not sold on finding a buyer to agree to take this on."

"Really? I thought you could talk anyone into anything," I say, my heart racing.

He smiles and raises his eyebrows at me, as if my words have hit a spot. He stands up and runs his hand through his hair, tossing the file onto his desk, then he turns around and leans against it, so he's facing me.

"Can you arrange a meeting with Benson for next week?" he asks.

"Of course," I say, ecstatic that he's actually considering my idea.

"Thanks. And can you type all of your notes up for me? I'll add to them and then get you to prepare a formal report that I can present to the board. I don't need it right away, by early next week is fine," he adds.

I nod as he stares at me. I hold his gaze and then stand up.

"Was there anything else?" I ask, so close to him that I could reach out and touch him.

"Nothing I can think of off the top of my head," he murmurs.

His eyes burn through me, but I hold his gaze, determined not to be the one to break contact. Self-doubt begins to creep in, but I push it away, because this moment is mine.

All I can think about is kissing him.

My heart pounds as I step forward. I put my hands against his chest and stand on my toes, so my mouth is almost on his. I swallow, feeling his warm breath on my lips. He doesn't move, so I tilt forward until my mouth is on his.

That's the only invitation he needs. With a growl, he lifts his hands to my face and presses his lips against mine, his lips roughly pressing against mine. I groan as his fingers rake my through hair, his mouth exploring mine.

He reaches behind me and untucks my shirt, slipping his hands underneath to explore my skin. My back arches at the feel of his touch, his lips still firmly against mine. He tastes amazing and I while can't get enough of him, I pull back, my lips parted slightly as I stare at him.

He smiles at me and reaches up, cradling my face.

"Is this the part where you tell me you have to go?" he asks.

I nod and take a deep breath, the touch of his fingers electric against my skin. He smiles and leans forward, planting a soft kiss on my lips. "That's probably a wise idea."

I turn around when I reach the door and look back. He smiles at me, still standing in the same spot that I left him. My heart races. I know I've started something that I might not be able to stop, but I don't regret kissing him. Not even for a second.

But I *am* going to regret leaving. Hell, I already do.

"I'll see you tomorrow, Alana."

If I wasn't in charge of organizing his meetings, I'd think Chase was avoiding me. It's three in the afternoon the day after we kissed, and I haven't seen him one all day. I came into work feeling great, but as the day drags on, my mood is slowly unraveling. All I can think about is kissing him. How it felt, what it means and where we go to from here. *Do I really want to get involved in something like this when I'm on the verge of breaking into something bigger than I've ever dreamed of?*

I wish I knew what the right answer was.

I throw myself into writing up my notes for Chase and then I search for more ammunition that he can use to convince a buyer it's a good deal. As it turns out, it's the perfect distraction, because I lose myself in the project for the next couple of hours, only stopping to make myself a coffee. Before I know it, it's five o'clock. I'm torn, because I'm so close to finishing that I just want to get it done, but Chase doesn't want me working late. I check his schedule. He's in a meeting for another two hours. I bite my lip and keep going.

He'll never even know if I stay back and get this done.

FINALLY, I'm done. I close my eyes and sigh. I'm completely exhausted, but it feels so good to finish, especially since I've found so much supporting evidence that even *I* could sell this. I open my eyes, jumping when I see Chase standing there. His amused smile turns into a frown when he glances at his watch.

Shit. He's back early.

"Why are you still here?" he asks, frowning at me. "It's nearly nine in the evening, Alana."

"It can't be that late." I gasp. I glance down at my phone. Nine o' six blinks back at me. *Fuck.* He's right. "I have no idea how that happened," I mutter.

I feel sick. He wouldn't fire me for working too hard, would he? But the look in his eyes tells me he wants to do *anything* but fire me.

"I'm sorry, I just wanted to get this done and..."

"I told you I didn't need that until next week," he says, leaning over to see what I'm working on. He picks it up and examines it. "Have you done more research?" he asks.

I nod. "I'm sorry, I just wanted to get it done because I was excited and I got carried away," I say, my face heating up.

Could I look any more like I'm trying to kiss his ass? I shiver at the thought of being that close to his cock. *His thick, stiff cock that I could feel pressing against my thigh yesterday when we kissed...*When *I* kissed *him.* I shudder. *I'm in way over my head.*

"Thank you, Alana," he says, still reading through my notes. He looks up at me suddenly. "You probably worked right through dinner. Are you hungry?" he asks.

I stare at him, not quite sure how to respond because there's only one thing I'm hungry for, and I'm pretty sure it's not on the menu.

"It's quite a simple question." He smirks when I don't reply. "It doesn't require *that* much thought, really."

"I *am* hungry." I admit, finding my words.

I keep thinking about that kiss and how good his lips felt against mine and how much I want to pick up where that left off.

"Okay, then grab your bag and let's go."

I don't have to be told twice. Jumping up, I throw my things in my bag and sling it over my shoulder, following him out the door.

"Where are we going?" I ask.

We make our way down the elevator to the parking lot. I follow him over to his car. He unlocks it, and I get inside, then he slides in to the driver's seat. He grins at me.

"My place. I'm cooking you dinner."

I burst out laughing. He looks slightly offended, so I shut my mouth.

"Oh...you're serious?" I ask.

"Of course, I am," he retorts. "It's how I unwind. Why do you sound so surprised about that?"

"I'm guess I'm surprised when *any* guy tells me he's cooking me dinner," I admit.

"Does that happen often?" He narrows his eyes.

"For your information, no, it doesn't." I flush.

"Good," he says. I hide a smile. I like it when he gets possessive of me.

I STAND IN THE KITCHEN, leaning against the counter as I watch him prepare dinner. He looks up at me and smiles. I shiver and smile back at him. I'm not even hungry—probably because I feel sick just being here again. I can't stop thinking about that night on the balcony. I glance over to it and blush, remembering how I felt when I realized it was *his* place.

"What are you thinking about?" he asks.

I snap back to reality and look up at him. He's staring at me, and the intense look in his eyes tells me he knows exactly what I was thinking about. I focus on the carrot he's chopping rather than him and don't answer.

"Would it be completely inappropriate for me to tell you how good you looked standing on my balcony that night?" he murmurs. I slowly raise my eyes until I'm staring into his. The way he's looking at me nearly enough to make me orgasm on its own. "I thought all my fucking dreams had come true."

My heart pounds. I don't know how to respond to that. I

open my mouth, but I can't seem to put my thoughts into words, because I have no idea what I'm thinking.

"Sorry," he says, with a chuckle. "If I'm making you uncomfortable, we can talk about how much I enjoyed you kissing me yesterday, instead?"

"No," I say with a little too much emphasis. "I mean... you're not making me uncomfortable." I glance down at the obvious erection showing through his pants. "Is that making *you* uncomfortable?" I ask boldly.

He lifts his eyebrows, chuckling as his eyes narrow. His eyes are full of such intensity that I feel naked when he looks at me. Without a word, he sets down the knife and slowly walks around the counter to where I stand. I can't breathe, but I hold my pose because I want this to be as much my show than his. I swallow, trying to calm my nerves, but it's hopeless. He's so close to me now, that I can smell his shampoo, and God, does it smell good. I grab the counter behind me for support as he moves even closer.

"Is this okay?" he murmurs.

I nod, because it's all I can manage. He puts his hands on my hips and roughly pulls me toward him, pressing my body against his. My heart is pounding out of control as he cups my chin and presses his lips against mine, somehow managing to be both firm and gentle.

I sigh and curl my tongue around his while we kiss, his lips so soft and warm against mine. He digs the hem of my shirt out from the band of my skirt, creeping his fingers underneath, along my bare skin. I shiver, my nipples hardening against his touch.

"*Oh*," I cry out. I laugh as he lifts me onto the counter, positioning himself between my legs. I feel his cock press against my panties and I smirk at how hard he is.

"Something funny?" he mutters.

Instead of waiting for an answer, he reaches behind me and clears space on the counter with the palm of his hand. Our dinner goes everywhere—all over the floor—but that's the last thing on his mind. He peels off my shirt, throwing it on the floor, then pushes my hair aside and kisses along my neck, until he reaches my breasts. He lowers my bra and closes his mouth around my nipple while I curl my legs around him, gently rocking myself against his erection.

I can't believe this is happening.

With his eyes on mine, he unbuttons my skirt and tugs it down. I lift my ass off the counter to make it easier for him, biting my lip when he takes my panties off too. I sit naked on the edge of his counter, with him nestled between my legs, his hands everywhere all over me.

"Lie back," he says.

I nod and lie my back down against the countertop. It's cold, but I barely notice because I'm too focused on how close his face is to my pussy. *God, I'm wet just thinking about him touching me there.* He smirks at me and kneels down so he's at just the right level, then he slides his tongue right along my entrance. His eyes don't leave mine, but I love that he's watching me. It's a huge turn-on.

"Holy crap," I gasp as he pushes his tongue inside me. I gasp and reach for his hair, my body flinching as his tongue fucks me. I grip hold of his hair and pull him closer.

"You're an impatient little thing," he chuckles.

He slows down again and circles his tongue around my clit. I groan, barely able to handle it. My legs tense as he slides his hand up over my stomach, holding me down. I gasp, my back arching as the tip of his tongue massages my clit. *Oh God.* I groan, crying out as I orgasm, my body shuddering as I hold his head against my entrance.

He lifts his head, his lips finding mine. I whimper as the taste of me on his mouth hits my senses. He pulls me to the edge of the counter. I smirk as I trail my hand down over his pants, lowering his zipper as I reach inside his pants to free his cock. I swallow, curling my fingers into a fist around his thick shaft, impressed with his size.

He groans, jumping at my touch. I look him in the eye as I slide my fist along his length. He reaches into his pocket and pulls out a condom, placing it between his teeth. I watch impatiently as he tears it open and rolls it over his erection, then he grips my hips, yanking me onto his length.

"Oh," I gasp, as he thrusts into me.

I wrap my arms around his neck, my pussy still throbbing from earlier, as he fills me. He grunts, bouncing me on his length, before lifting me into his arms and carrying me over to the couch. He sits down, with me on his lap, kissing me while he thrusts inside me.

"Fuck that feels good," I whisper as I slide up and down his shaft.

He grunts in response, his hand exploring my back while his tongue rolls around my nipples. He bites down, making me shriek, just as my body begins to convulse for a second time.

"Oh God, I'm coming," I mutter.

My breathing shallows as I wrap my arms around his neck, my thighs tensing as I ride him. He groans and bucks his hips against me hard as he releases. I press my mouth against his while he's deep inside me, my pussy contracting around him.

Gasping, I roll off him and lay on the couch, sweaty and out of breath. He takes my hand and kisses it, pulling me into his arms. I giggle, not sure what I'm finding so amusing. He raises his eyebrows at me, which makes me laugh harder.

"Glad you find fucking me that amusing," he says with a glint in his eyes.

"Sorry," I say, still catching my breath. "I'm just..." I shake my head. "I can't believe that actually happened."

"Give me half hour and it'll happen again," he chuckles. I blush, not sure if he's serious or not.

We lay there, talking about everything and nothing for what feels like hours. I stifle a yawn, which makes me glance back into the kitchen at the clock on the wall. It's nearly eleven. I frown, wondering where the time went. We haven't even eaten dinner.

"I guess we should order a pizza or something," he says, reading my mind.

"Pizza would be nice," I grin.

It's nearly midnight by the time we finish eating. I'm so tired and still shocked about what happened earlier, but I know I need to go home. I get to my feet and smile shyly at him.

What happens now? Do I kiss him again?

I hate that awkward feeling of not knowing where things stand. He takes my hand, making the decision for me as he pulls me into his arms. My heart races as he presses his lips against mine, our tongues clashing.

"I better go," I mumble.

"You could stay here," he suggests. I'm so tempted to say yes, but all my things are back home, and it would just make getting to work tomorrow an even bigger rush.

"No. I better get home. Thanks though," I say, "and sorry I ruined your dinner."

He chuckles. "You can ruin my dinner anytime. Let me drive you home."

I wave him off. "Go to bed. I can catch a cab." I lean up and give him another kiss on the lips, my cheeks flushing. "See you tomorrow..." I glance at my phone. "Today, later at work."

"I'd say sleep well, but I'm sure thoughts of me will be keeping you awake all night," he teases.

I make a face at him, wishing he wasn't so damn right.

CHAPTER TEN
CHASE

"CAN WE TALK?"

I raise my eyebrows and nod.

"Sure. Close the door and sit down."

I watch as she walks back over to the door and carefully closes it, then she wanders back over to my desk and sits down. I wait for her to speak, even though I already know this is going to be about last night.

If she's anything like me, she was probably awake half the night thinking about it. And by thinking about it, I mean with my hand wrapped tightly around my cock and my fist sliding at full speed. God, she was incredible. And the taste of her pussy...

I shift in my seat, because it's all I can do not to throw her onto my desk right now and fuck her again.

"What did you want to talk about?" I gently coax her.

"Us," she admits. "I just wanted to set some boundaries.

I enjoyed last night. A *lot*," she adds, blushing. "But I want to make sure when I'm at work, we keep things professional."

I nod, all my fantasies of fucking her over my desk evaporating into the air around me.

"Of course," I say, adjusting my collar. "That sounds perfectly reasonable."

She breathes out, looking visibly relieved.

"Okay, good. I better let you get ready for your next meeting then," she says, getting to her feet.

I nod and reach over to grab her Benson notes that I've finished reading through.

"When you get a chance, if you can type this up for me?" I say, handing it to her.

She nods, glancing down at it. Her brow creases. "You haven't added anything to this, yet though," she frowns.

"I didn't need to," I say honestly. "You've pretty much covered every angle I would have."

"Really?" she smiles.

I nod. "You should be proud of yourself. This is great work."

"Thanks," she says. "That means a lot to hear you say that..."

She stands up quickly, her arm catching a stack of folders near the edge of my desk. She gasps and watches them scatter to the floor.

"Shit," she mutters.

I shift in my seat, trying to ease my erection as she crouches on the ground, ass up in my face, collecting the files. She turns around and plonks them on my desk.

"Sorry about that," she says.

She smiles at me, her cheeks flushed with color like she's just been fucked.

Hard. By me. Just like last night.

"Was there anything else?"

I glance at my watch and groan. Fifteen minutes before my meeting is due to start.

Come on.

This keeping work and us separate bullshit is killing me already.

"You're looking a little stressed there," she says, keeping a straight face. "Have you ever thought about trying meditation?"

"Fuck meditation," I growl. I reach out and grab her arm, swinging her onto my lap. She gasps as I force one leg over both of mine so she's straddling me. "I'll show you how I relax."

I slip my hand under her skirt and push aside her panties. She groans and tenses her legs as I slide my finger inside her. I kiss her on the mouth, my lips pressing against hers as my finger circles her clit. She wraps her arms around my neck, burying her face against my chest.

With a grunt, I lift her off my lap and spin her around, laying her face down on my desk. I hitch up her skirt and peel down her panties, then lower my zipper. She giggles, turning her head to the side as I reach inside and grip my cock. She spreads her legs apart as I line myself up at her pussy, before pumping my length into her. She groans, her body flinching as I fuck her hard, thrusting my shaft deeper and faster into her wetness.

"Fuck," she hisses, grabbing hold of the edge of my desk to steady herself.

I groan, my hands tightening around her hips as I shoot my load inside her. She whimpers, her body twitching as she comes with me inside her.

"Oh God," she moans, her cries getting louder.

Gasping, I pull out of her and sit back in my chair, scooping her into my lap. She giggles as I kiss her, then climbs out of my embrace to straighten herself up. I watch her, amused and still turned on by the sight of her as she slides her panties back up her thighs, then nudges her skirt back into place

"So much for the no sex at work rule," she says, narrowing her eyes at me.

"Ah, so this was *my* fault?" I chuckle. "You're such a cock tease."

"And you're such a romantic," she says.

"I am," I agree. "Which is why I'm taking you out tonight."

"Where?" She asks.

"Dinner," I say with a smile.

"No."

"No?" I laugh, not sure if she's being serious or not. "And do I get a reason as to why not?"

"Because you promised to cook me dinner last night," she explains, her eyes twinkling.

"Ah, so want you me to *cook* for you?" I rub my jaw and consider her request. "Okay, fine. My place at seven."

"Good," she says with a content nod. She steps forward and kisses me, then rushes out of my office. "By the way," she says, poking her head back in. "Don't think I've forgotten about my internship."

I sink back in my chair and smirk. I hadn't forgotten about our arrangement, but I'm not sure if I like or if I hate the idea of not having her around me as much.

I met with the board of Benson Industries yesterday and I have to say, Alana really had an eye when it came to choosing them as her pick. I know she's got a boner for analytics, and while I'm sure that played a big part in her reaching the conclusion that she did, I think she'd be wasted in that department. I'm thinking bigger things for her, but it's something I can't do overnight.

I just need to put the idea of this internship off for a *little* while longer.

Right on seven, she knocks on my door.

I whistle as I walk over to answer it, hoping I look cool calm and collected, which is the complete opposite to the kind of evening I'm having in the kitchen. It started off with the potatoes, which I set fire to when I forgot the water in the pot. I found it kind of amusing. Unfortunately the fire department who turned up after the smoke alarm and sprinkler system went off in the hallway of the building, didn't share my view. Then I realized I'd forgotten the main ingredient in the dressing for my salmon. Why is it everything has to go wrong the one time I boast about my skills in the kitchen? *I guess it's better than it happening in the bedroom, because that would be a real disaster.*

I open the door Alana stands there, holding up the lemon that I texted her to get for me.

"This is a first," she says with a smile. "I've never been asked to bring my own lemon on a date before."

"Because it never been on a real date with a *man* before," I tease her. "I bet your wondering where I want to put *that*," I add.

She laughs and then sniffs the air.

"Is something burning?" she asks, glancing around.

"Just my dignity."

She looks at me curiously and walks inside, my gaze following her. She looks stunning as always, in a short black shirt and dusky pink lace top. I shut the door and walk back over to the kitchen.

She leans against the counter and watches me as I prep the salmon.

"Let's see how much I can fuck this up," I joke.

"You're not buckling under the pressure, are you?" she teases. She glances at the salmon and frowns. "I'm expecting something exceptional. You did build yourself up quite a bit," she reminds me. I laugh and wipe my forehead. She's right. I am feeling the pressure because I want tonight to go well.

"And here I was thinking that you were the master at keeping calm."

I narrow my eyes at her. She's enjoying this way too much.

"So...would now be a good time to tell you I don't like salmon?" she asks. My head snaps up and I look at her in horror. She holds her hands up to her face. "I'm sorry, I was going to try and tough it out, but even the smell of it is making me want to hurl."

"It's fine," I say with a groan.

I scoop up the fish and put it into a bag and back into the fridge and then wash my hands. *I'm sure I'll see the funny side of this in about a decade.* She walks over to me, wrapping her arms around my neck and kisses me.

"I feel like I ruined your dinner for a second time," she says. She frowns, but her eyes are sparkling. I kiss her on the nose and chuckle.

"No, I managed that all on my own," I respond dryly. "Okay, so now what?" I grumble.

I fucked up on the potatoes and she doesn't like salmon. Dinner isn't looking all that great. She glances at the bowl of beans soaking on the counter. Her eyes meet mine and we both laugh.

"I love beans," she says brightly.

After we finish yet another pizza—with a side serving of beans, I lean back in my chair, glad that part of the evening is over. All tonight has achieved so far is to give me a complex over cooking for her.

"Who would've thought pizza and beans could be a thing?"

she teases. I frown, pretty sure she's making fun of me. "But seriously, thank you for going to so much trouble. And at least you can still redeem yourself and impress me with dessert," she offers, her eyes twinkling.

Dessert? *Well, shit.*

Her eyes widen and then she laughs.

"Chase, I'm disappointed in you. Given your reputation with women, you *have* to know that you can't ask a girl over for dinner and not supply dessert."

I reach over and grip hold of the legs of her chair, dragging her closer to me, then I lift her hand to my mouth and kiss it softly.

"Maybe I have other things on my mind for dessert," I mumble. "But first, can I tempt you with a glass of wine?" I ask.

"Yes please," she says.

I stand up and walk over to the kitchen to grab a bottle of wine and two glasses I have ready for us. I pour the our drinks and then motion for her to join me.

"Out there?" she says with a laugh, when I lead her towards the balcony. I chuckle and hand her wine to her.

"When it's not six in the morning and you're wearing clothes, it's actually quite nice out here," I say, opening the door.

She follows me outside. I notice her eyes dart across to my neighbors balcony, and then she relaxes. She looks up and gazes out over the skyline.

"I didn't notice those beautiful lights before," she breathes.

I nod. "It's pretty spectacular. To be honest, I didn't notice them either, last time. The view right in front of me was much more beautiful."

She laughs and turns around to face me. I lean in and kiss her softly on the lips, then I take her wine and set both our drinks down on the ground. I sit down and gesture for her to join me.

"In your lap?" she giggles.

"Trust me, it's romantic," I reply.

She sinks into my arms, chuckling as I wrap my arms around her waist. She tilts her head against me and closes her eyes, breathing in as she smiles.

"I could stay out here all night," she murmurs.

"You almost did," I remind her.

She giggles. "Let's see if you can get through one night without mentioning the balcony incident."

"That would involve you having to stay here with me, all night long," I point out. She flushes. "Not that I'd complain about that."

She turns her head toward me and kisses me, pressing her lips hard onto mine. Then she gets onto her knees and repositions herself so she's facing me. She stares into my eyes while I stroke her hair. I smile and kiss her again, my lips massaging against hers. My hand moves slowly over her back. I groan, loving the way her body reacts to me.

She straddles me, her body rubbing against mine, making me hard as fuck. But she always has me hard. All she has to do is look at me and I'm gone. I run my finger around her face and down between her breasts, until I reach the first button on her shirt. I undo it, not dragging my eyes away from hers. I take my time undoing all of them, until her shirt just hangs open flapping gently in the wind. I curve my arm around her waist and thrust her towards me, my fingers exploring her back.

She kisses me wrapping her arms around my neck. I stand up and so does she. I lift her into my arms and turn her around, leaning her against the wall. She groans as I kiss her, my lips slowly moving their way down her neck. I reach for her breasts and thrust her bra down to reveal her nipples, then I close my mouth around them. I suck, curling my tongue around them until they're hard. Still kissing her, I walk around to the other side of the balcony, to the door that leads into my bedroom. I yank it open and walk inside, throwing her down on the bed. I climb on top of her, my hands roaming over her body as I kiss her neck. With one hand, I attempt to unbutton my shirt. I eventually manage it and shrug it off.

I strip off my pants and my boxers, then kneel against the edge of the bed and drag her toward me. She leans back on her hands, lifting her ass off the bed as I gently roll her skirt down over her thighs. She watches me as I part her legs and slide her closer to me, then I run my tongue over the outside of her panties.

She gasps, arching her back as she falls back onto the bed, her hands clutching at the sheets beneath her. With a growl, I reach into my bedside table and snatch up a condom, then position myself over her.

I break the packet open and roll it onto my length. With one hand on my cock, I drive myself inside her. She groans, her body jolting up the bed against my thrusts. I wrap my arm around her neck to keep her steady, kissing her as I enter her.

"Harder," she gasps, pressing her mouth against mine. I grunt as I drive my cock into her, each thrust with more intensity than the last.

I fling her leg over my shoulder to give me deeper range. She cries out, reaching above her head to clutch onto the bed post. My hands move all over her body and so does my tongue. I can't get enough of her.

"Fuck," I groan, my cock throbbing as I release, shooting hard inside her.

"Oh, *Oh, God,*" she gasps.

Her mouth falls open as she tilts her head back. She grabs hold of my hand, squeezing it as she comes. She whimpers, her body tensing as her legs tighten around my neck.

Pulling out, I collapse next to her on the bed, chuckling softly.

She turns to me and half heartedly raises her eyebrows.

I shrug. "That's what I call dessert," I grin. She chuckles and then rolls onto her side to study me. "You certainly satisfy my sweet tooth," I add, tilting her mouth up to mine.

She laughs, her lips spreading in a smile as she rolls her eyes and pretends that comment didn't make her heart flutter. She reaches for my hand, entwining his fingers in mine.

"Can I ask you something?" she says, her gaze dropping to her fingers as they crawl along my side.

"Sure," I say. My nerves kick into gear because her tone is terrifying me.

She takes a deep breath and then lifts her eyes to meet mine. I tense, sensing the seriousness of what she wants to ask me.

"When's your birthday?" she whispers.

I stare at her, shocked. "Pardon?"

She smiles. "I don't know when your birthday is. Or what your favorite TV show is. I don't even know what your favorite food is." She releases a deep sigh. "Or whether you're allergic to dogs."

"Allergic to *dogs*?" I chuckle. "Do you have any idea how nervous I was at what you were going to ask me?"

She shrugs. "I don't know, the way I look at it, they're the kind of things that differentiate something casual from..." Her voice trails off as her face goes red.

I chuckle. "From what?" I prompt her, kissing her lips. She swats me away when I try to tickle her.

"Look, I'm not trying to label this as anything, because it is what it is, but if I'm honest? I hope that this is more than just a casual hook up."

"Well I'm not here for a cheap thrill, if that's what you're getting at," I assure her.

I roll her over onto me and kiss her again. She smiles at me as I stroke her hair. Hearing that she's open to this going thing somewhere actually makes me feel pretty good. I still don't know what this is, but I do know that I like being with her. That's a good start, right?

"Okay," I say as she straddles me. "We're going to play a

game. You're going to ask me questions and when I answer, I'm going to kiss you."

She laughs. "That doesn't sound like much of a game. How do I win? And what do I get when I win?"

I pull her arms so she's lying on top of me and kiss her slowly.

"You get me," I tell her.

She laughs. "Okay. Birthday?"

"February nineteenth," I say. I kiss her softly on the mouth, rolling my tongue around hers. She smiles, then narrows her eyes.

"How old were you when you lost your virginity?" she asks.

I have to think about that one. "Fifteen I think."

"You *think*?" she giggles.

"It was a long time ago," I defend myself. Then I kiss her again. *I'm enjoying this game.* "When do I get to ask the questions?" I ask. "This doesn't seem very fair. You're learning all about me and I still know nothing about you."

She sighs. "Fine. We will alternate."

We spend the few hours just laying on my bed, talking about everything and nothing. I can add to the list of things I know about Alana that she hates basketball, and that she loves swimming, Vietnamese food and every pretty much every clichéd chick flick where the girl gets the guy in the end.

"But what about action?" I ask her. She frowns at me. "Die Hard? Die Harder? Under Siege? Universal Soldier?" I say.

She narrows her eyes at me. "Are you making these up?"

I chuckle. I'm going to have to do some serious educating of her pop history knowledge.

I'm not even game enough to ask her if she's heard of Star Wars.

Before I know it, our evening is over and I'm walking her to the door. She wraps her arms around my neck and kisses me. I grin, loving the feel of her lips on mine. She looks into my eyes and something sparks inside me.

"Thank you for a wonderful evening," she says. She takes my hand and entwines her fingers in mine, then lifts her gaze to meet mine again. "You're full of surprises, Chase Winston. I like it. Keep them coming."

We kiss again, then I watch as she disappears around the corner. I smile as I close the door. It was an exceptional night. I wander back down to the living room and pick up my phone, which I find on the floor under the kitchen table. I catch sight of an unread message, so I open it.

> ***Josh:*** *Second suit fitting this weekend sometime? Let me know when suits.* (*See? Still got the humor*).

I smile in spite of myself, but my amusement quickly dissipates when I remember what it's for and who I've told my brother my plus one will be. I'm not sure how to handle this. I want to come right out and tell her that we've been invited to my brother's wedding, but delving into the truth feels like a whole lot of baggage she might not be ready for. The last thing I want to do is scare her off.

But the other side of this is that I've told Josh she's coming to the wedding so I can't turn up without her. As stupid as it sounds, I need to show both of him and Casey that I've moved on. I want them to be in awe of me, not pity me.

I'll just see how things go. There's no point in telling her when I don't even know what this is. She's still my assistant. Taking her away for a function isn't beyond reasonable.

At least, that's what I'm telling myself.

CHAPTER ELEVEN
ALANA

> ***Chase:*** *Wear that white shirt of yours that's a little bit see through. Even though I can't touch, I like to look.*

I ROLL OVER, unable to wipe the smile off my face. It's been a permanent fixture for the last two weeks, pretty much from when the Chase and me thing started happening. It feels like we've been seeing each other for so much longer than that. I have to pinch myself just so I know I'm not dreaming. I'm sure I'm going to wake up and realize the only real thing was me arriving on his balcony.

I don't know how, but we've managed to keep things mostly professional while we're at work for an entire week. I'm impressed that he's been so good at respecting what I want—with one or two slip ups along the way.

It's Tuesday morning and after spending the night at

Chase's, I arrive to work early. I walk inside and over to the elevators, getting there at the exact same time that Peyton does. She smiles at me and then glances away. I shift on my feet as I wait for the doors to open. It takes forever, leaving us in the middle of an awkward silence that neither of us seems to know how to fill.

"I miss you," she finally says, frowning at me.

"I miss you too," I whisper.

My heart races, because I've been dying to tell her about Chase, but I just didn't feel like I could go to her like I used to. The old me would've been on the phone to her the moment I left his house, but the reality is, we haven't spoken properly in weeks.

"You moved on with my replacement." I say the word like it's dirty. She laughs and shakes her head.

"What? Are you kidding me? No way, Lanna! I mean she's nice and all that, but she's no you," she says, a dopey grin on her face.

"Then why do you stop talking every time I walk into the room?" I ask, frowning.

"That's not me, it's her," Peyton exclaims. "Think about it from her perspective. She's new here, and you're her boss. I think she's just afraid that you're going to yell at her or something. I just shut up out of politeness."

I frown. *I guess that kind of makes sense.*

"Come here," Peyton says, throwing her arms around me. I hug my friend, glad to have her back. "How about we catch up?"

"Shopping after work tomorrow?" I suggest with a smile. I know she won't say no to that and it's something we used to do a lot. "I've got something to tell you."

Peyton's eyes widen "And unless the news is you're boning Chase, I don't want to hear it." Her eyes widen. "Why are you blushing? *Alana*?" She gasps and throws her arms around me.

"Shh," I say, laughing. "I'll tell you everything, but not now."

"Then when?" she demands.

"Tomorrow?" I suggest. "Shopping, like we used to?"

She squeals and nods. "You're on."

CHASE CALLS me into the office the moment I sit down at my desk. I glance down at my shirt and smirk, then undo the top button. Just because I want to keep things professional doesn't mean I don't like teasing him. I knock gently on his door before walking in. He looks up, smiling when he sees it's me.

"You got my message, I see," he mutters approvingly.

I walk over to him, until I'm close enough to see that he's hard. I shiver, wanting nothing more than to climb onto his lap and ride him.

"I did," I say. "To be honest, I never even realized it was that transparent. I'll never wear this in front of my father again." Chase groans and covers his face with his hands. I laugh. "What?"

"Thank you for curing my erection," he growls. I laugh again.

"Sorry. So, did you just want to see me in this shirt, or...?" I tease him.

"I'd prefer to see it *off* you, given the choice, but for your information, I have a perfectly valid reason for bringing you in here," he murmurs. "We're going away for the weekend. I have an important function that I need you to attend with me."

"Really?" I say, trying to remain calm. I love the idea of spending a few days away with him. "What function is it?"

"Just...a function."

I raise my eyebrows at him. "That's all I get?"

"You need more than that?" he says with a grin. "Come over here, and I'll give you a *lot* more."

"More *information*, thank you," I say with a smirk. "Such as where we're going and how we're getting there. What I need to pack? Do I need something dressy? Or is it more corporate? You know, details," I tease.

"Right, sorry," he says, rubbing the back of his neck.

I study him closely. *Is it just me, or is he acting weird?*

"The function is black tie, so something dressy. We will be leaving late Friday afternoon. And it's in Florida, so we'll be flying over there. There will be separate rooms, of course, at the hotel." He pauses and raises his eyebrows. "If you *want* separate rooms, that is."

"Separate rooms would be great," I say with a grin. *If only to torture him.* "So, what's this function for?" I ask. I'm still confused, because it's sounds like an odd way to seal a takeover.

"It's just to do with a merger I've been working on for a while," he says. He reaches into his wallet again for his trusty credit card. "Can I leave you to pick up my suit? And get yourself something to wear that I'll want to tear off you later, when we're alone," he adds, trying to pull me back into his embrace. I laugh and step back, giving him a stern look as I shake my head.

"Work at work and play at home. You know the rules," I say, shaking my finger at him. "I'll see you later, Mr. Winston," I purr as I back out of the room.

"Tease," he murmurs, his eyes flashing as stares at me.

I PICK up his suit on my way home. My dress I'll figure out tomorrow when shopping with Peyton. The first thing I do when I get home is pour myself a glass of wine. I walk over to the couch, slipping off my heels along the way and sit down. The second my ass hits the seat, my phone rings. I groan and glance back to the kitchen counter, where my bag sits with my phone inside it. I reluctantly get up and walk over there, fumbling through my things until I grasp it. I smile when I see a message from Chase.

> ***Chase:*** *So what do I need to do to tempt you over here?*
>
> ***Me:*** *How about you come over here?*

When he doesn't respond after a few minutes, I toss my phone on the couch and then decide to take a quick shower, just in case he does decide to come over. No sooner than I've peeled my clothes off and stepped under the water, there's a knock on my door.

Shit. I jump out and grab my bathrobe, throwing it on, then I race out to the living room. I check my phone on the way to the door, wondering how he got here so fast. But there is still no response from him. *Huh. Maybe it's Peyton.* I swing open the door, shocked to see Chase grinning at me.

"You look surprised to see me," he comments. I flush. "You flush a lot, Alana. What's up with that?"

"I was expecting a little more notice," I grumble, ignoring his question. He leans closer to peer inside.

"So you could tidy the place up a little?" he guesses. "I'm not judging, but you'd think you'd do that *before* inviting someone over."

"You know, it's not too late for me to slam the door in your face," I say sweetly. I gasp as he puts his hands around my waist and spins me around, so he's inside. "I guess it is now," he replies, a glint in his eyes.

My heart pounds when I remember I'm naked under my robe. He looks me over, like he's wondering the same thing.

"Would you like a drink?" I ask, keen to change the subject.

It's just an excuse to get away from him for a moment so I can catch my breath. He shrugs and follows me as I walk into the kitchen. My hands shake as I pour him a glass of wine. I slide it across the counter to him and then walk back over to the couch for mine.

I sit down. He sits down next to me. Any closer and he'd be in my lap.

"As we were discussing," he comments. "Why do you embarrass so easily?"

"It's just around you, and probably because your always so inappropriate," I retort.

He nods. "I guess I am."

He leans forward and picks up photo on the coffee table.

"You and your father?" he asks. I nod. "You look happy," he says.

I shake my head and laugh.

"That's not true, actually. This picture was taken right after he said I couldn't go on the roller coaster for the fifth time, so I was anything but happy. He dragged me into that photo booth while I was fighting back tears."

Chase smirks. "I guess it shows how much a photo can lie, doesn't it?"

I nod. "I guess it's does."

"So," he says, glancing at me. "Since we've established how inappropriate I can be, I'm just going to come right out and ask you if you're naked under that robe," he murmurs.

My heart races as I stare him and of course I feel my face going red.

"Why don't you find out?" I say boldly.

"Stand up," he orders me.

I do as he tells me and turn around, so I'm facing him. Still sitting down, he reaches forward and places his hands between my knees. He slowly rides his hand up until I gasp as his fingers touch my bare pussy. I swallow, my knees almost giving way.

"I'd say that's a yes, but we need to be sure."

With his other hand, he releases the tie around my waist, letting it swing open. He smiles as it slides over my shoulders and off me, leaving me naked.

"Come here," he orders.

I sit straddled on his lap. He keeps his eyes on me as he leans forward and presses his lips against mine. Then he lowers his mouth and closes it around one nipple and then the other. I gasp as he sucks and flicks his tongue in circles until they're stiff.

I wrap my arms around his neck and guide his lips to mine, kissing him deeply and then I reach down and lower and unbuckle his pants. He fumbles in his pocket for a condom while I wrap my hands around his cock, sliding my fist along his length. I take the wrapper from him and tear it open, then roll it over his length.

I position myself over him and slide down hard, gasping as he penetrates me. He growls as I kiss him, rocking myself back and forth against him as he fucks me. He groans, his hands roaming my body, exploring me everywhere. I gasp, riding him harder and faster until my body begins to tremble. Panting, I ride him harder, my lips pressed against his, until I feel like I'm going to explode.

I roll off him and fall onto the couch into his arms. I smile as he kisses my head, both of us catching our breath. I shiver as he strokes my arm. He kisses me again, the feel of his lips on mine incredible.

"Just so you know, I came over to hang out and talk. I was determined not to do this," he murmurs.

"Good work, then," I tease. "What changed?"

"You," he admits. "Seeing you standing there, knowing there was nothing under that robe..." He shakes his head. "It was too much." He pauses for a moment. "I want to take you out tomorrow night."

"Out where?" I laugh.

"On a date," he says, sounding vulnerable.

"Okay then," I say, I smiles shyly.

"I'll pick you up at seven," he says.

"I'll be ready," I murmur.

CHAPTER TWELVE
CHASE

I TAKE my time getting ready, deciding on a pair of suit pants and a dark grey sweater. I stare at my reflection in the mirror and then I run my hands through my hair, roughly styling it into place. It's been a long time since I've been out on a date. I've been with women, sure, but never like this. I haven't been with someone I can potentially see a future with since Casey. It's scary, because in order to see where this can go, I have to put myself out there, where I risk getting hurt again.

Again.

God, am I actually admitting that losing Casey hurt me?

I know it did, but knowing it and admitting it to myself are two different things. For two years after we separated, she still occupied my thoughts. Lately though, it's not Casey I've been thinking about. Hell, I hadn't thought about Casey at *all* in two whole weeks.

Things have been going well, but I feel like I'm waiting for things to go wrong. I think that's part of why I want to take her out tonight. I like her, and I want her to know that this is more than just sex. Though the sex is fucking mind-blowing.

I've booked us into one of the top restaurants in Boston, where we will be served a seven-course degustation menu prepared by one of the top chefs in the country, who happens to be an old college friend of mine. I'm actually kind of nervous about it. It's like I'm worried that if she gets to know me too well, she might decide this isn't worth it. *Or maybe you're worried she'll find out everything you're hiding.* I frown, realizing how anxious that makes me.

Maybe I like her even more than I thought.

RIGHT ON SEVEN, I knock on her door. I hear movement on the other side, but it's a moment before she opens it. She smiles at me. I take her hand and kiss it.

"You look stunning," I say to her.

"Thanks. You look pretty good yourself," she grins. "So, where are we going?"

"Have you heard of Kingston?" I ask her. I already know the answer will be yes.

She laughs at my question. "Everyone has heard of Kingston," she scoffs. Her eyes widen. "Don't tell me you got us reservations there?" she gasps. "*How*?"

"What can I say? I know people," I grin. "So, shall we go?"

She nods. I take her hand and we walk to my car. I help her in and then shut the door, walking around the front to the driver's side. She smiles at me as I get in and buckle in my belt. I start the car and drive off, the excitement in my stomach beginning to give way to nerves.

We drive through the city in the direction of the water, which the restaurant overlooks. I pull to a stop outside it and get out, handing the attendant my keys. Alana waits until I open the door for her and extend my hand.

Alana clutches onto my arm as we walk through the restaurant, her eyes wide with excitement. I glance down at her short, dark purple dress, my throat constricting. Why did I have to make tonight about everything other than sex? Fucking her is all I can think about, seeing her in that dress, but I'm determined to show her that this is more just about sex.

"Holy shit," she hisses, tugging at my arm. "I'm pretty sure that's Kayne West over there.

I turn and smirk. "Yeah, that's him," I say with a chuckle.

"You seem less impressed than I am," she comments, narrowing her eyes playfully. "Which I'm assuming means you've been here before?"

I nod as the waiter leads us to our table.

"Once or twice," I grin.

Once or twice being nearly every month.

Not only do I like the food, but I'm also friends with the owner. We went to college together, so we catch up and have lunch every now and then.

I sit down. Alana looks around, the smile never leaving her face. Then she glances around, like she's lost something.

"What have you lost?" I ask her curiously.

"Nothing," she mutters. "I was just looking for the menu."

"There is no menu," I say with a smile. "Degustation means the chef decides what to serve. It comes out over seven courses. Small courses," I add when her eyes widen.

"How have I never heard of this is before?" she says, shaking her head. "This is perfect. I hate making decisions. I'm terrible when it comes to choosing when I have more than one option."

"I'm having trouble believing that," I say with a grin.

"It's true. Three weeks later and I'll still be trying to work out the pros and cons."

"That's not necessarily a bad thing," I say with a smile.

"It is when I miss out on the things I want because of it," she replies.

"It's funny, because I would've thought the opposite about you," I say. "I see you as calculated and organized."

She shakes her head vigorously. "No way. I've always been like this. I used to drive my father crazy when I was younger. He'd asked me to choose somewhere to go out for dinner and I'd still be deciding on the drive there. One time we went on a vacation and I was still booking the accommodation a hour before we arrived."

I chuckle, studying her with amusement.

"What?" she grins. "I'm a sucker for making sure I'm getting the best deal."

The first course comes out. I smirk when I see what it is. Escargot. I', not the biggest fan, but I'm more interested in seeing her reaction. I'm pretty confident her reaction isn't going to be positive. The waiter places her plate in front of her. She leans forward and breathes in. "God that smells amazing," she murmurs. "I love escargot," she adds, when I can't take my eyes off her.

"Wow. You actually know what they are," I grin. "I'm impressed."

"Believe it or not, I've been known to fine dine on one or two occasions," she teases. "I had them nearly every day when I was in Paris."

"Paris?" I repeat. The shocks keep coming.

She nods. "I spent four weeks there right after I finished high school. It was my way of proving to myself that I could handle being on my own," she explains.

"So you went alone?" I say, surprised. I've never been a seventeen year old girl, but I'd imagine that's a pretty big deal. "I'm even more impressed. There's so much more to you than I realized," I add.

"Because I'm indecisive and I've been to Paris alone?" she jokes. "Which, by the way, was a hard decision to make. It came down to Rome, Paris and Berlin, so I drew one out of a hat." Her eyes sparkle. I'm not sure if she's joking or serious. "So," she says, raising her eyebrows. "When do I learn more about Chase?"

"What you want to know?" I say.

She smiles, her eyes locking on mine. "What you want to tell me?"

Everything.

The next course comes out before I can answer her question. I smirk when I see that it's chicken livers. I shake my head, because this one sure to test her. I didn't know what the menu was, but Luke knew that I was bringing a date, so I'm pretty sure this is his way of messing with me.

Without missing a beat she leans forward and scoops up a forkful of the delicate meat, before putting it into her mouth. She smiles, a dreamy expression forming on her face. I shake my head.

"Do you know what they are?" I chuckle.

"Chicken livers?" she says. She looks at me and raises her eyebrows. "Anyone would think that you were trying to trip me up, Mr. Winston."

"Hey, in my defense I had no idea what the menu would be," I say.

"Uh huh. Sure you didn't," she replies, narrowing her eyes.

The rest of the courses aren't nearly as risky, and before I know it, we just finished number six. Alana narrows her eyes at me.

"Is dessert one of these courses?" She asks playfully. "Because if not, you owe me something sweet. The same rule applies, whether you cook for me or take me out, Mr. Winston."

"Gladly," I chuckle. "Ice cream on the way home it is, then. I'd offer you the choice between ice cream and waffles, but I wouldn't want to put you in a hard position." I wet my lips and stare into her eyes. "At least, not *that* one."

"How thoughtful of you," she retorts.

After dinner, we walk along the river, enjoying the ice cream I promised her, while continuing to get to know one another. Then out of nowhere, she curses loudly. I glance at her and raise my eyebrows.

"I left my jacket back in the restaurant," she explains. "It's one of my favorites," she adds, a pained expression on her face. "Would you mind...?"

"Going back and getting it for you?" I guess. I glance back up the steep hill we'd just walked down and smile. "Of course. I'll be right back."

I lean over and kiss her before I start the trek back uphill to the restaurant.

I'm out of breath and sweating bucketloads by the time I reach the front doors. I look everywhere, for the missing jacket, but I can't find it. It's literally vanished. After nearly twenty minutes of searching and an argument with the waiter, I give up and walk back to where I left her, to break the news.

"I'm sorry," I begin. Then I frown and eye her suspiciously. "That jacket you're wearing looks *awfully* similar to the one you just sent me on a marathon to retrieve," I comment.

She glances down, her eyes widening.

"How on *earth* did that happen?" she exclaims. She stares

at me innocently, but her eyes are laughing at me. "I guess I must have had it right here all along and I didn't even know it."

"This wouldn't happen to be payback for that time with my shirts, would it?" I growl, wrapping my arms around her waist. She laughs as I thrust her against me. I kiss her, my mouth ravaging her neck. "That was very disrespectful of you, Alana," I mutter. "I might have to teach you a thing or two about manners."

"Oh, really?" she says, smiling at me. "You know you deserved that," she says.

She presses her mouth onto mine, kissing me slowly. I sigh as she pulls away, my lips still tingling from her touch.

Glancing at my watch, I wince. It's late—much later than I was expecting. I have no idea where the time has gone, but I've had fun. Even more than I'd expected. I take her hand and walk her back to my car.

We get in, neither of us saying much for most of the drive back. But it's not a bad silence. It's one of those where you're happy and content just letting things be what they want to be. I glance over at her and smile as we pull into her street.

I pull up outside her apartment complex and I insist on walking her to her door. The moment we reach it, I lift her face to mine and kiss her, pressing my mouth against hers. She sighs, closing her eyes until I pull away. I study her expression, taking everything I can about her in.

"Do you want to come in?" she asks shyly.

I smile at her. "More than anything," I admit, my heart pounding. "But I won't."

I lean over and kiss her again on the lips, this time slowly and tenderly, savoring every little touch. She sighs as we part, her eyes closed, her eyebrows slightly raised. I chuckle and kiss her again, then let go of her hand. I want to go in there so badly, but I also want to show her that I can be more than just about sex. Even if it fucking kills me in the process.

"See you tomorrow, Alana. Sweet dreams."

CHAPTER THIRTEEN
ALANA

"DETAILS," Peyton demands, when I meet her at the mall on Thursday after work. "You owe me two fucking weeks' worth of Chase fucking the cobwebs out of your vagina details, woman."

"Honestly, I don't even know what to tell you," I giggle. "Where do I even start?"

"Um, the beginning? How the fuck did it progress from nothing to *this*? Who started it?" she makes a face. "Stupid question. He obviously did—" She stops and gawks at me when she realizes I'm shaking my head. "You started it? *You*?"

"Don't sound so surprised," I reply indignantly. "I can be bold and daring when I want to be."

"Really?" she says. "Because prior to this, the most daring thing I've seen you do is wear red with orange." She shakes her head, still coming to terms with how much she's missed. "So what happened?"

"We were in his office, and I kissed him."

"Just a kiss?" she presses, her eyes twinkling. "How was it? Was that when you..." She winks at me as she raises her arms and sways her hips, until I reach out and slap her playfully.

"No, it was just a kiss and then I left," I explain. "Then the next day, I finished work late and he insisted on making me dinner—"

"He made you *dinner*?" she growls, her eyes wide.

I laugh. "Well, not quite that time. He *intended* on making me dinner."

"What the hell does that even mean?" she says, shaking her head.

"It means dinner ended up all over the floor because he fucked me on his kitchen counter instead," I say, my face heating.

Her eyes widen as she clasps her hand over her mouth. She stares at me in shock for a few moments and then she shakes her head.

"Get the hell out," she gasps, clapping her hand over her mouth. "Are you *messing* with me? Oh my God, you're serious? On his kitchen counter?" she gasps. She throws her arms around my neck, hugging me, while kissing me on the cheek. "That's so fucking hot and *amazing*. How was he? I mean, I don't want the details, but was it good?" she asks.

I sigh, a dazed smile on my face. "I can't even put into words how amazing it was."

"And this has been going on for two weeks? I can't believe you kept this all to yourself!"

I nod. "He's incredible, Pey. We've been together nearly every night. And it's not just sex. He took me out for dinner last night. We talk about all sorts of things..."

I sigh. It's hard to put into words how I feel when I'm around him.

"And now I get to spend the whole weekend with him."

"What do you mean?" she asks.

"He's taking me on a business trip. Three nights alone—well, if you don't count the other couple of hundred attendees who'll be there," I joke.

"Holy crap, is that why we're shopping?" she gasps.

"Yes," I say with an excited nod. "I need something sexy, but classy for a function this Sunday."

Without another word, she marches me into a small boutique called Game.

"Forget sexy," she declares. "We can do better than that. What you need is blow his mind, make him want to fuck you in the middle of the conference, kind of sexy." She looks around, a determined look on her face. "And if we're going to find it anywhere, it will be in this shop."

I nod, her passion and enthusiasm spurring me on. I'm pumped and ready to shop.

"Let's do this."

Ten dresses later, and I'm done. I sit down outside the boutique, deflated, because I'm never going to find the right dress. I might as well just wear a hessian sack. Hell, he'd probably find that sexy, anyway. Peyton is still in the store, refusing to give up, but I know it's a lost cause.

I glance around me, looking for options, and then I see it. The perfect dress. My heart races as I stand up. It's on a mannequin in the window of a boutique across the way. I slowly walk over there, just as Peyton walks out of Game.

"I'm sorry. I feel like I've let you down. Stupid store," Peyton grumbles. I turn around and grab her by the shoulders, leading her over to the window. Her mouth drops open. She nods.

"Yes. *Yes*," she cries, her eyes glassy. "That's perfect, Lanna!"

I race inside and search for the dress, but I can't find it anywhere. An assistant finally walks over to help us when Peyton begins to get hysterical. I point at the dress, too out of breath to speak, from going through rack after rack looking for that dress.

"I'm sorry. That's the last one," she says.

"What size is it?" Peyton demands.

"I'm not sure. Let me check."

We both watch, holding our breath as she climbs up into the window display and unzips the dress. She looks back over to us.

"It's a four," she announces.

"*Yes*," I practically cheer. Peyton throws her arms around me.

"Don't get too excited until I try it on," I say to her. She rolls her eyes, but nods.

"It's going to be perfect."

I hope she's right.

I take it into the dressing room and peel off my clothes and then slide it up over my body. It's a perfect fit, but that doesn't mean it looks any good. I finally find the courage to lift my eyes and look at my reflection in the mirror. I'm stunned by what I see. The blue silk looks almost purple in some light, and it just clings to my body. It drapes softly against the floor, but with the right heels, the length will be perfect. I reach up and touch where the dress dips dangerously low into my cleavage. The amount of breast I'm showing is daring, but the conservative length of the dress kind of makes it okay.

Holy shit. That can't be me.

My heart races. It really is perfect. I can't even move, it's so perfect.

"Are you ready?" I call out to Peyton.

"I've been ready for the last ten minutes," she grumbles. "Hurry up already."

I pull back the door and walk out. Peyton gasps. She shakes her head, speechless. I don't think I've ever seen Peyton speechless in all the time I've known her.

"You're crying," I say to her, laughing. She shakes her head and wipes away tears. "Seriously, maybe you're the one that needs to get laid," I giggle.

"Trust me, I've been getting a lot of it lately, and I've got all the allergies to prove it," she smirks.

"So how are things going with Mr. Vet?" I tease, referring to the guy she's been seeing for a few months now. How he still doesn't know that she's allergic to dogs, I have no idea.

She smiles. "Really well," she admits. "He's so nice, Lanna. I think I need to tell him that I'm allergic to his giant dogs, though."

"If things are going that well, you'll work around it," I say. She nods but doesn't look convinced. *This guy must really love his dogs.*

"Back to you and that dress. Please tell me you're getting it?" she pleads. She grabs the tag, her eyes widening when she sees the price. "On second thought, you might need to take out a loan first," she whistles.

"Good thing I have this, then," I say, flashing the credit card at her.

"Is that Chase's?" she gasps. "He gave that to you?" I nod. She shakes her head. "Okay, now I'm *really* jealous."

I giggle and link my arm through hers as we walk over to the counter.

I TREAT Peyton to a smoothie to say thanks for helping me shop. She races to the bathroom while I wait for our drinks. I stand beside the counter, feeling happier than I have in a long time. I feel like nothing can bring me down. I glance over to see if Peyton is coming back and my heart stops. It's not Peyton that I see though. It's Dani and Aaron. I turn around, praying they don't see me and try to crouch down around the side of the counter, where I'm pretty sure I'm not supposed to be.

"What are you doing?"

I look up and see Peyton standing there, shaking her head.

She's right. What am I doing?

I can't believe what I'm about to do, but there's no doubt in my mind that I need to do it. I stand up and straighten myself up and then I walk over in their direction. They don't notice me until I'm right in front of them.

Dani looks up first. She pales when she sees me standing there. I see her grip tighten on Aaron's wrist. He turns around, looking visibly sick when he sees me.

"Alana," he mutters. "Hey. How are you?"

"Good," I say, not believing for a second that he actually cares.

"Uh, how are you? Having a nice evening shopping..." His voice trails off. It takes everything for me not to laugh in his face. That's all he has to say to me?

Dani hesitates. "I'm glad we ran into you," she says softly. "I've been meaning to call you since..." She stops and swallows before continuing. "I really want to apologize for what happened. I just want you to know I never meant to hurt you."

"The fact that you didn't *want* to hurt me doesn't change the fact that you did," I say. With a rush of confidence, I for myself to go on. "I want you to know something." I look her dead in the eye and then Aaron. "You both hurt me. I trusted you. I trusted both of you and you betrayed me in the worst possible way. You have no idea how that made me feel or how long it took to get over both of you. You hurt the most," I say to Dani. "We shared our whole lives together. Guys come and go, but I thought you'd be the friend I'd still have in my life when I turned eighty." Tears roll down her cheeks as I keep looking her in the eye. "I hope he was worth it. I hope he was worth ruining our friendship over, because that's what you did."

"Alana, please," she whispers, covering her mouth with her hand. She wipes away tears and puts her hand out, but I back away. "No," I say. "I won't back down just so that you feel better. I need you to know how much you broke me, so that I can move on." I sigh. "I didn't come over here to make a scene, or yell at you, or any of that. I don't care about anything, other than the fact that just being able to walk over here and say this to your face."

Dani looks down. She runs her hand over her stomach and that's when I notice the bump.

"When are you due?" I say quietly. She looks surprised and then embarrassed.

"I'm six months tomorrow," she whispers.

"Congratulations," I say. "I hope you're happy. I really do."

I turn and walk away, feeling like the weight of the world is on my shoulders. All I want to do is fall into a heap and cry, but I don't, because what I did took courage and I need to be proud of that. It took a lot of damn courage. I shake my head and laugh as I near Peyton. She stares at me with wide eyes and then wraps her around arms around me, kissing me on the cheek over and over again.

"I'm so proud of you right now," she whispers.

"Yeah," I say. "I'm pretty proud of myself, too," I admit.

I take a deep breath, still feeling shaky. I can't believe that I did that. Last week—hell, even yesterday I wouldn't have had the courage to do that. I never got the closure that I needed from that relationship, and I think that's part of what's been holding me back. That and my remarkable ability to pick really bad men. My mind wanders to Chase.

Maybe all that is finally changing.

"THANKS AGAIN FOR HELPING ME OUT." I say to Peyton, as she pulls up outside my building.

It's been a long day and I'm exhausted. Running into Aaron and Dani has made a whole heap of emotions resurface that I thought I'd dealt with a long time ago.

"Are you okay? She asks, giving my arm a sympathetic squeeze.

I nod. "I think so? You know, it's funny. For seven months, just the idea of seeing them made me feel sick, but tonight, I not only faced them and told them what I needed to, I did it on *my* terms." I smile. "I think I actually feel pretty damn amazing."

"Good." She grins, giving me a hug. "And just so you know, it took everything for me not to march over there and sucker punch that bitch."

"I'm glad you didn't," I grin.

"So am I. I'm proud of you for standing up to them, but now, just put it behind you and move on. You owe that to yourself." I nod, knowing that she's right. "Besides," she says, pausing for effect. "You have more important things to worry about. Or should I say *people*."

I roll my eyes wishing I hadn't told her who I was going away with. Of course, she would've figured it out pretty quickly when neither of us were at work tomorrow.

"Stop it." I say to her with a mock frown.

"Stop what?" she says, her dark eyes widening.

"*That*," I groan. "Smiling every time I say his name."

"Come on." Peyton squeals and grabs my arm. "It's perfect! You know it's perfect and when he sees you in that dress, he's not going to be able to keep his hands off you."

"I'm going now," I groan, opening the door.

"Bye!" She says, practically hanging out the window as I walk across the sidewalk to the front door. "Don't do anything I wouldn't do, and make sure you use protection," she calls out. "Herpes ruins lives, you know!"

I cringe as the doorman grins at me.

CHAPTER FOURTEEN
CHASE

I PULL up outside Alana's house right on time. I glance at my phone, wondering if I should call her to let her know that I'm here. *I'll give her five minutes, and if she's not out by then, I'll call her.* No sooner than the thought leaves my head, she walks through the doors. I blast my horn and she waves and starts walking in my direction.

I let out a low growl, because God, she looks fucking gorgeous. I feel a twinge of guilt, but I shrug it off. I've almost managed to convince myself that it's not that a big deal that I haven't told her the real reason for this trip. We're going to my brother's wedding. So, what? It's not that different from going to a business function, right? It's bound to be just as exciting.

Though I'm not sure she'll see things that way when she finds out.

I pop the trunk and she throws her bags in, then slams it shut. She jumps in the car and smiles at me, her lips slightly parting as she pants, out of breath. I clear my throat and shift in my seat, focusing on anything other than her, because all I can think about is her sitting on my desk, panting like that as I slide my cock inside her. I groan and shift in my seat, my dick throbbing.

"So," she says clipping her seat belt in. "Tell me more about this merger."

Shit. She's caught me off guard. I didn't think I'd need a back story prepared, because I figured she'd just go with it.

"It's two unities coming together as one. I've known both of them for a very long time, so they personally requested that I be part of this." I'm pretty impressed with how good I made that sound, and none of it was a lie.

Maybe I should offer to write Josh's vows for him.

"Nice," she says with a smile. "I figured that it must be important for you to take time out of your weekend and pay me triple time."

"Triple?" I say raising my eyebrows.

She shrugs. "I think that's fair, don't you? You didn't think that just because we're seeing each other that I'd go easy on you, did you?"

"Fine. Triple it is, I guess." I nod, hiding my smirk.

The last thing I want is her going easy on me.

I DRIVE into the airport and park the car in the short-term parking section, then we carry our bags and check in for our flight. Every time I glance at her, I get this unfamiliar twinge of guilt rushing through me. I can tell myself as much as I like that I don't feel bad about lying to her, but the truth is, it's all I can think about.

It's not like she's not going to figure it out the second we get there, anyway. It's just I know by then it will be too late for her *not* to go through with pretending to be my girlfriend.

I rub my head and sigh. I don't know why I didn't just ask her if she'd come with me in the first place. It's not that big a jump from what we're doing right now, anyway. But I couldn't risk even the *slightest* chance of her saying no.

"You booked us in first class?" she gasps as we board the plane. I nod, amused at how much she's loving this. "Oh my God. I've never flown *anywhere* first class."

She sighs as she sinks into her oversized reclining armchair and closes her eyes. I watch her for a moment and then sit down next to her.

"If you want another first, the bathroom's just back there." I say with a wink. Her eyes widen. "I'm joking," I say with a chuckle. "Well, unless you're interested, that is?"

I glance at her bare thigh and resist the urge to reach out and touch it.

"We both know how daring you are," I add with a sly grin. "Seducing your boss, and all that."

"I seduced *you*?" she growls, her face going red. "Hold on, *you* were totally the instigator."

"Come on," I say with a laugh. "You act like you're some innocent little lamb. Even if you didn't make the first move, you set the idea in motion. You're the one who got me thinking about you in that way. The way you spoke about sucking my cock and then turning up at my house? Is it any wonder I couldn't stop thinking about you?"

"You couldn't?" she asks with a smile.

"You sound surprised, but it's exactly what you wanted. You manipulated me," I say with a grin. I'm teasing her, but it's exactly how I feel. I've been completely pussy whipped.

She bites her lip and looks down, a smile creeping across her lips. Then she glances behind us and back at me. Her eyes are laced with something I can't quite put my finger on. She stands up and walks down the aisle, turning back after a few steps.

Her eyes sparkle. "So, are you coming, or not?"

I jump up. "With any luck, I will be in a minute," I mutter.

The stall is much crampier than I was expecting, but we somehow make it work. I stare at her breasts as I lift her shirt over her head, then reach behind her back to unclasp her bra. I nod approvingly, taking her nipple in my mouth as I unbutton her jeans. I roll them down over her thighs, while she kicks off her shoes.

She removes her jeans while I thread her pink, lacey panties down over her legs. All I can smell is her sweet pussy, and it's driving me crazy. I wrap my arms around her and press my lips against hers. She groans, pressing her body against me as my fingers circle her back.

"Hang on," she says, pulling back enough to narrow her eyes at me. "How come I'm naked and you're still completely dressed?"

"Because there's something incredibly hot about fucking you, naked, in this tiny stall, while I'm still fully clothed," I say. The plane jerks forward suddenly, sending me crashing into her.

"I think the question I should be asking, is how long we have before we take off," she whispers, her face going pale. I chuckle, and she frowns at me. "Yeah, it's all right for you. I'm the one who's going to be sprawled out face down in the aisle out there, butt naked."

"Relax. I'm sure we've got plenty of time," I say with a laugh.

I lower my zip and reach inside my pants to free my very hard cock. She glances down and smiles as she wraps her fist around my shaft, sliding her fingers up and down my length as she presses her lips against mine. I groan and nudge her legs further apart. She takes the hint and positions her foot halfway up the wall, giving me much better access.

"Fuck, you're so wet," I mutter, sliding a finger inside her. She whimpers as I alternate between massaging her clit and thrusting my finger into her pussy. I lift my hand to my mouth and suck on my finger. "You taste pretty good too," I mutter.

I get down on my knees and bury my tongue in her pussy. She gasps, covering her mouth with her arm to smother her screams. I take that as a challenge and work harder and faster, determined to get a very vocal reaction out of her. I lift her onto my face and suck her clit, wrapping my arms around her thighs for better control. She groans, thrashing around in my arms as she does everything she can to be quiet.

I smirk when she looks down and meets my eyes, then I slow things right down, focusing only on her clit. I suck it until it's stiff, then bite down on it, before drawing circles around it with my tongue. She's so close. I run my fingers up over her stomach, to her breasts, and roll her nipples between my fingers. She moans, her thighs clenching around my face as she flexes her hands against the wall, bracing herself.

"Holy shit," she gasps, panting softly as I slide my tongue back and forth over her clit. "Oh God, please stop. I can't. Oh God, I can't..." Her voice trails off as I fuck her sweet pussy with my tongue. I'm relentless, and moments later, her body begins to spasm. "Oh God," she cries out.

She groans loudly as she comes on my face. I grunt, ignoring the glower she's directing my way as she rides out the last of her orgasm. When she's done, I let her off me, laughing as she reaches over and slaps me on the arm.

"Hey," I say with a grin. "I think what you mean is thank you."

"Because now I have to go out there where everyone now knows exactly what you were doing to me in here?" she growls. "You're lucky I'm not spiteful, or I'd be doing the same thing to you."

I look down at my stiff cock and shrug.

"Knock yourself out."

She opens her mouth to respond, just as a call is put out over the intercom to prepare for takeoff.

"Sorry. Looks like we're out of time," she says, smiling sweetly at me as she quickly dresses.

"Yeah, I bet you're sorry," I murmur, watching her step back into her panties and roll them up over her thighs.

This is certainly going to be an interesting trip.

WE GET off the plane and catch a cab to the hotel. It's the same location as the wedding, so I'm nervous about running into someone who knows me. I glance over at Alana. This thing with her wasn't supposed to happen. I wasn't planning on taking her to this wedding either, until Josh cornered me into naming a companion, but at that point, nothing had happened between us, so I figured it wouldn't be a problem. Now, it all just feels complicated.

As we walk into the hotel, Alana looks around the lobby, her eyes wide. It's a five-star place, like I always stay in, but the look on her face has me wondering if we've struck another first. She grabs my arm and pulls me aside, a serious expression on her face.

"So we're on the same page, this is a business trip, right? Meaning, we keep things professional?" she says.

"Like on the plane?" She glares at me. "Okay," I agree, swallowing a laugh. "But this isn't work."

"No, but it's work *related*. I don't want everyone at work thinking I got my promotion by sleeping with you, and the same goes for here. People will already be wondering if I'm sleeping with you. I don't want to give them proof."

"They'll only get that if you're as loud as you were on the plane," I murmur. She glares at me, so I stop. "Okay. Point taken, and if that's what you want. No sex. We even have separate rooms, so you don't need to worry about the temptation being too much."

I strut off over to the reception desk to check us in before she can respond to that.

"I'm sorry, sir. You said that you booked two rooms?" the attendant asks after I give her my name. She frowns at the computer screen.

"Yes," I say, frowning. I know where this is going, and I can't believe it. Alana isn't going to believe this is a mistake. She'll think I had this planned. With everything else that's going to piss her off, I don't need this too.

"I'm so sorry, sir, but you only have the one room showing up on our system. We don't have anything else available, either. There's a big wedding on this weekend."

"I know," I say, gritting my teeth. "I'm part of it."

"It's a double room if that helps at all," she says with an unnaturally wide smile.

Sighing, I nod. It's not like I have any choice other than to agree. *At least we have separate beds.* It wasn't like I intend to let her use her room anyway, but I wanted her to know she had the option. And now with this no sex at work rule she's implemented, I want it to be her decision to break it.

Our relationship has developed so fast that neither of us has really had time to process it. For all I know, she regrets sleeping with me in the first place. That wasn't the impression I got on the plane, but still...

"Fine. If I can have the keys now, it would be *greatly* appreciated," I say with fake gratitude.

I take the key and turn around, scanning the room for Alana. I spot her sitting over by the indoor water fountain, a look of dismay on her face. I watch her as she glances around, making sure nobody is looking before she tosses a coin into the water. I laugh and walk over there.

"What exactly are you doing?" I say with a grin.

"Oh my *God*, would you look at this?" she hisses. "Who the hell puts a water fountain in the middle of the lobby?"

"I'm glad you're enjoying it," I say, amused. "But you do realize that it's not a wishing well, right?"

"I was just making sure," she says defensively, her cheeks flushing.

"What did you wish for?" I ask, looking at her closely.

"Nothing," she mutters, refusing to look at me. "Can we go to our rooms now?" she asks, changing the subject.

"Sure, but there's, uh, a slight issue with the *rooms*," I say. She raises her eyebrows at me. "I promise you, this isn't some elaborate scheme to tempt you into my bed, but they've lost one of my room reservations."

"Convenient," she says. She narrows her eyes at me and frowns. "So, you expect me to share a *bed* with you?"

"No, of course not," I growl, shaking my head. "There are two beds. It's just the room we're sharing. But, if that makes you uncomfortable, I can sleep in the lobby, or something." I say. I glance around, looking for a good spot to sleep.

"Oh, don't be stupid." she says rolling her eyes, "You think

I'd have a problem sharing a room with you after what happened on the plane? And your kitchen counter?" she says with a giggle. "And everywhere else you've fucked me?"

"I didn't want to assume," I reply honestly. I also didn't want her to think I wasn't taking seriously what she'd said earlier.

"It's fine," she says. "I meant what I said about keeping things professional, but I think we can manage to share a room together. Of course, if you're thinking that only *one* of those beds is going to be used, you're going to be disappointed."

"Not at all," I say without missing a beat. "I have great plans to fuck you senseless in both of those beds when you finally come to terms with the fact that you can't resist me. I figure we can use one for morning sex and the other for evening sex. Mix things up a bit."

"I..." Her voice fades away as she stares at me, open-mouthed.

"See? You can't even think of a way to respond to that," I say as I grab our bags and walk over to the elevators.

She joins me a few seconds later, still not saying anything. Every now and then I feel the weight of her stare as she looks at me. When I finally catch her, I wink at her. She flushes and looks away. I tap my foot impatiently, and when the doors finally open, I'm happy to see the car is empty. I step in and smile at her.

"Coming in?" I ask. She hesitates. *She doesn't trust herself to be alone with me.*

If she can't even handle herself alone in an elevator with

me, how is she going to handle sleeping in the same room as me? She steps inside, shooting me a glare, before facing away from me.

"This keeping things professional rule while at work is *your* call, remember. I'm more than happy to bend the rules." I raise my eyebrows and grin as my gaze slides down over her ass. "Among other things."

"God, you infuriate me sometimes," she mutters.

Her eyes blazing, she turns around and walks over to where I'm standing. She presses herself against me, her mouth almost on mine. I groan as she reaches down and rubs her palm over my cock.

Holy shit, that feels good.

I cradle her face and press my mouth against hers, kissing her passionately. My heart pounds, because being with her is everything. I feel like her intention was to wind me up and show me that *she* is in charge, only now she can't break away, and I can't either. I'm resisting the urge just to rip her clothes off and drive myself into her right here and now. My hands creep towards the button on her jeans, when suddenly, the doors fly open.

We both spin around to see an elderly couple waiting to get in. Alana flushes and looks down while I smother a laugh. The lady hesitantly steps into the car, but her companion puts his arm out to stop her. He looks from Alana to me, alarm in his eyes. His expression has me seconds away from being in hysterics.

"He was just checking something in my eye," Alana mumbles desperately.

Her comment sets me off. Alana glares at me, which makes me laugh harder. She would've been so much better off not saying anything at all.

"Stop laughing," she hisses.

"I can't," I gasp through fits of laughter.

In the end, they decide to wait for the next elevator.

"Asshole," Alana hisses when the doors close. She glares at me. "You made me look like a fool. *Again.*"

"I'm sorry, but you made yourself look like a fool." I chuckle.

I reach for her hand, pulling her closer to me. She narrows her eyes, but then her expression softens, and she relents, letting me wrap my arms around her.

"And all because you can't keep your hands off me."

I OPEN the door to our room and let her walk inside first. She looks around, examining everything from the minibar selections to the bathroom amenities. I check the message that's flashing on the phone. It's the reception desk, letting me know they found us a second room.

"You'll be relieved to know that you don't have to share my room with me, after all," I say when I find Alana in the bedroom.

"What do you mean?" she asks, frowning.

Is it just me, or does she look disappointed about that?

"The message on the phone was the reception desk, letting us know that they found another room," I say. I run my fingers down over her arm and cock my head slightly. "If you like, we can pretend that message never came through..."

She looks up as I lean down and kiss her. I cup her neck, pressing my lips against hers, whilst guiding her back toward the bed. She sits down, lying back as I hover over her. She sighs as I lift up her shirt and kiss along her stomach.

Knock, knock, knock.

I roll over onto my back and groan while she stifles a giggle.

"Are you fucking *kidding* me?" I groan. It's like nobody wants me to get off today.

"We can ignore them," she suggests, a fire in her eyes. "It's just going to be the hotel letting us know about the room."

We both lie there, completely still, hoping they go away. Just when I think they have, the knocking starts again.

"Chase, are you in there? It's Josh."

"Shit." I mumble, jumping to my feet.

"Josh?" she repeats with a frown. "Who's Josh?"

I glance back at Alana who's looking at me, confused. I know the questions it's going to raise, but I *have* to be honest with her.

"Josh...is my brother."

CHAPTER FIFTEEN
ALANA

"YOUR BROTHER IS at your work function? What's he doing here?" I ask, confused.

Chase stands up and buttons up his shirt. He sighs and rubs his forehead, before turning back to me.

"It's a long story," he mumbles. He glances back at the door, hinting that he doesn't have time to go into it now. "I'm sorry, Alana. Do you mind...?"

"Sure, of course." I straighten myself up and then grab my phone. "It's your room, after all," I add, walking toward the door.

He half-heartedly tries to stop me but gives up when I leave the room. I brush past Josh without a word. I can immediately see the resemblance between the two of them. Josh is like a younger, more innocent version of his brother. I disappear down the hallway before either of them can say anything.

OUTSIDE I BREATHE out and shake my head, trying to work out what is going on. I'm so confused. Why would his brother be here at a work-related event? Is he in the property sector too? Maybe he's part of the merger? It's possible, but why wouldn't Chase have mentioned it? Come to think of it, he's never mentioned his brother before at all. I guess that's not that unusual, but I still can't help feeling like I'm missing something. I just wish I knew what.

I WALK a few blocks down from the hotel toward the beach, where I stumble across a funky looking coffee shop. I wander in and order myself a drink, sitting down at one of the tables along the window while I wait. I pull out my phone and try calling Peyton. I'm disappointed when she doesn't answer, and then my insecurities set in. *Maybe she's out with her new friend.* I shake off the jealousy refusing to let myself fall into that trap. *Besides, I have enough to worry about with Chase.*

The waitress brings over my coffee. I smile at her and then glance over at the rowdy group of girls sitting at the table over from mine, wishing they would talk a bit quieter. My head is pounding and they're making it worse. I know jet lag from a three-hour flight isn't really a thing, but I feel like crap.

What I'd been *hoping* to do was have a nap before doing whatever it was we had to do tonight, but I guess that's not gonna happen now. It probably wouldn't have happened without the interruption from Josh either, but still. *Unless I go back to the hotel and ask for that other room.*

I'm so tempted... I shake my head, thinking about Chase. The way his lips felt on mine when he kissed me, the way he smiled at me when I say something he found cute... I groan.

That's the thing; I don't *want* another room. I want to sleep in the same room as him. I want to fall asleep in his arms, preferably after he's sufficiently fucked every part of my body.

"Right. So, Chase is Josh's brother. He's like a sexier, naughtier version of Josh."

My ears prick up. I glance back at the table of girls, hoping I'm subtle enough with my eavesdropping. The blonde at the table laughs at something the redhead just said.

"I know I shouldn't say that, considering what he did to Casey, but that doesn't change how sexy he is. Though I *am* shocked he even showed up here."

I frown, my heart racing. *How do they know Josh and Chase?* And why do I feel like I've been played?

"I know," exclaims the brunette next to her. She's wearing way too much makeup, so when she moves her mouth, it all cracks. "I can't believe that he had the nerve to show up for the wedding. I mean Jesus, have some respect for poor Casey."

"I heard he brought along some chick, too," the blonde says, rolling her eyes, "Just to rub salt into the wound, but I guess that's perfect Chase behavior, isn't it?"

I haven't even finished, but I get up and quickly leave. I know they have no idea who I am, but I'm seconds away from bursting into tears in the middle of a crowded coffee shop. I race back to the hotel and walk up to the reception desk, hoping I look confident enough to pull this off.

"Hello," I say, smiling again. "You left a message with my boss, Chase Winston, that you found me a room? I'm here for the key."

"Right, yes. We're *very* sorry about the mix-up. I hope it didn't cause too much trouble for you." She hands me a key. "It's conveniently located right next to your boss's room. You've even got an interconnecting door."

"Fantastic," I say, plastering a smile on my face.

Something I definitely don't plan on using.

I TAKE the key and head back upstairs, praying to God that I don't run into him. I need time to think, and I can't do that with him in my face. I let myself into my room, locking the door behind me. I can faintly hear voices on the other side of the wall, near the bed. My heart races as I walk over there. Am I really about to listen through a wall to try and overhear the conversation between my boss and his brother?

God, what would Peyton say if she could see me now? Okay, so she would probably be cheering me on, but that's beside the point. It's not like I can hear anything anyway. I give up and lie down on the bed, closing my eyes. *Maybe if I fall asleep, I might wake up and discover that this is all a bad dream.*

I ROLL over and open my eyes, jumping up about a meter in the air when I see Chase sitting on the bed next to me. He smirks at me. I blink back at him. At least my headache is gone.

"Hey sleepyhead," he says.

I sit up, resting back against the pillows. I frown at him.

"How did you get in here?"

"I went down to reception and they told me you collected the other room key," he says with a shrug. "They mentioned it was an interconnecting room and they asked if we wanted they key for that too. I said yes," he explains. I glare at him. "Sorry, I guess I should've asked you first if that was okay. I won't come in here if you don't want me to," he adds, frowning.

"Why are we here, Chase?" I ask him.

He looks at me, bewildered. Then something clicks in his eyes, and I *know* that he knows that I know. He takes a deep breath and releases it slowly.

"We're here for my brother's wedding," he says quietly.

"What?" I say. I laugh at how ridiculous that sounds. "Why would you tell me this is a business trip? Hell, why did you even bring me at all?"

He stands up and walks over to the fridge, bending down to examine the contents. He pulls out a tiny bottle of scotch and twists the cap off, necking it down, then he walks back over the bed and sits down.

"Sorry, I needed something to be able to get this out."

"Get what out?" I ask impatiently. "What could you possibly say that makes this—"

"My brother is marrying my ex-wife," he says, cutting me off.

I stare at him, shocked. "He's *what*?" I gasp.

He nods, looking down at his hands. I sit forward and wait

for him to continue, in the hope he might answer the million questions whirling around in my head.

"I was married to Casey for five years," he begins. "We started having problems pretty early on, and by the end of our first year together, I think we both knew that things were over."

"So, what happened?" I ask. "I mean how did you get from that to her marrying your *brother*?" I close my eyes, struggling to get my head around this.

"I guess we'd pretty much separated by that point." he says. He doesn't sound that certain, but I let him continue. "She didn't really have anyone else she could turn to, so she turned to him. Apparently, that's where it started. The next thing I know they're a couple and he's calling me to let me know that he's marrying her."

"Wow, that's pretty full on." I mutter. I feel sorry for him, and I'm at a loss at what to say. "And you're okay with that?" I ask. He shrugs and finally looks at me.

"I want them to be happy, so I'm fine with it," he says. "I guess that's why I'm here, to show that I'm okay with it."

"Okay. But why am *I* here?" I ask softly.

He flushes. "Because I didn't want to be the guy who turned up at his brother's and ex-wife's wedding alone?"

"And that's it?" I say with a frown. "No more surprises? Because I still feel like there's something you're not telling me. I mean, how do people know about me?" I ask.

"Who knows about you?" he asks, looking worried.

Worried I'm going to find something out, maybe?

"I overheard a group of people talking about you guys in the coffee shop and they mentioned me," I explain.

"I *may* have hinted to Josh that you were coming," he mutters. He runs his hand through his hair.

"And what exactly did you say about me?" I ask.

"That you were, uh, my girlfriend?" he says. His tone rises at the end, making it sound like a question.

"Your girlfriend?" I say with laugh. I swallow, one more question poised on my tongue. "When did you tell your brother this?" I ask. "Before we first got together, or after?"

"Before," he mumbles.

A pit forms in my stomach. *Is that why he started this thing with me? To make it easier to get what he needed?*

"Please don't think that this has anything to do with us," he says, reading my thoughts.

"It doesn't?" I ask, my heart racing. "It's *awfully* convenient, then, isn't it? I bet you thought that you could get around telling me at *all* if you made me feel like you were interested in me for five minutes."

"Alana, please, just hear me out, you're overreacting—"

"I'm overreacting?" I growl. I shake my head "Fine, I'll be your date for this stupid wedding, because you're paying me to, but after that? You're nothing more than my boss."

He sighs and covers his face with his hands, looking like he needs to tell me something else.

"What is it?" I bark.

"Josh kind of invited us out for dinner."

"So, go," I say, crossing my arms over my chest.

"You're supposed to be my girlfriend. He's expecting you to be there," he says helplessly.

"Jesus," I groan. I roll over, burying my face in the pillows. "Fine." I snap. "I'll go to your stupid dinner." He nods, looking relieved. "Now if you don't mind, I'd like some time to myself."

"Sure," he nods. I watch him as he walks to the door, calling out to him just before he leaves. He turns around, his expression hopeful.

"I really appreciate that you are paying me quadruple time for this weekend," I say sweetly.

He frowns and mumbles something under his breath, before nodding.

"Fine," he says through gritted teeth.

"THAT FUCKING ASSHOLE!" Peyton rages when I tell her what just happened.

"I'm gonna kill him. I'll fly over there and kill the guy."

"Calm down, I'm handling it," I say. I lie back on my bed staring at the ceiling, talking to my friend. "The worst thing was I was really starting to believe that he was actually feeling something for me."

"I'm so sorry. You're not having much luck with guys, are you?" she asks.

"I wasn't having much luck *before* him and Jake," I say with a frown. "But this is just ridiculous."

"At least you're getting a free mini-vacation," she says weakly.

"But what's the point when I have to spend all my time with him? I can't even look at another guy." *Not that I even want to look at other guys.* "We've got connecting rooms, for God's sake."

"I'm sorry. Do you want me to come over? I could make this fun," she offers. I giggle, tempted to say yes and make Chase pay for both of us.

"I bet you could, but no. I can handle this. At least he *is* paying me well for it."

"I hope you're milking it for all it's worth," Peyton says, agreeing.

I laugh. "Trust me, I am."

RIGHT THROUGH DINNER, I'm the perfect girlfriend in front of his friends and brother, but the second we're alone, even for just a moment, I make sure he knows that I'm still angry as hell. He's edgy and nervous, glancing at me every five seconds, like he thinks I'm just waiting for the perfect moment to reveal everything.

I frown and stab at my chicken as I listen to him chat with Casey. I've gathered that she is the ex-wife, because I knew her name already and because the moment I saw her, I wanted to go all Jerry Springer on her. *Okay, so maybe there's a little anger built up inside me.*

I'm trying my best to pretend that I don't care, but every time she laughs at something he says, my heart dies just a little bit more. I look up and watch him talk to her. If I didn't know better, I'd think that they were friends, not two people who went through a messy break-up. I feel sick just thinking about it.

Why am I so jealous? He's just another asshole I can add to my list. God knows I should be used to it by now. I glance back down and push my plate away, suddenly not very hungry. I look back up and see he's staring at me. My heart races as the tears begin to well.

"I can't do this. I'm sorry," I mumble.

I push my chair back and stand up, rushing outside. I don't want to lose it in front of him or his little group, but if I don't get out of there fast, the tears were going to flow.

I lean against the wall of the restaurant, enjoying the cool breeze as it hits my face. I close my eyes, slowly feeling better. I walk across the road toward the water, staring up at the star-studded sky. I'm marveling at how beautiful it is, but it's short-lived when I glance over and see him walking toward me. I shake my head, the anger rising all over again.

"Can't I get five minutes by myself?" I ask him, angrily.

"I was just checking that you're okay," he says, his voice quiet.

"Well, I'm *not* okay," I say, glaring at him. "I hate that you've put me in this position, and I hate that I actually *like* you."

I stalk across the sand and over to the water. He's right behind me, but I don't care. He reaches out and grabs my wrist, spinning me around. I glare at him trying to shrug his hold of me, but he's too strong.

"Let go of me," I cry out. "You don't care about anyone but yourself."

"No, not until you listen to me," he growls.

"Fine. What do you have to say to me?" I say, stepping back to keep a safe distance between us.

"I'm sorry, okay? I'm sorry I didn't tell you where we were really going, and I'm sorry that you think my feelings for you aren't genuine." He shakes his head and laughs bitterly. "I get that your angry, but I don't know what else you want me to say."

"How about that you're sorry that you made me fall for you?" I say, my voice barely a whisper.

I feel like an idiot. *This is all my fault.* He probably thought I was up for a casual fling. He didn't know how much I was beginning to like him.

"That wasn't about this at *all*," he says, his eyes begging me to listen. "Since I broke up with Casey nearly two years ago, she's all I've ever thought about."

"I so don't need to hear this," I say, covering my ears. He reaches over and grabs ahold of my wrists, holding them against his chest, forcing me to hear him out.

"Well, you're going to," he whispers hoarsely. "At first, I thought you might be a good little distraction from my problems. But as you wound your way deeper into my world, I started to realize how much I actually *liked* having you around."

I stare at him, my heart racing. I'm not sure whether I

believe him or not. What if this is all just an act so I don't fall apart and reveal everything to his precious friends?

"I haven't thought about Casey in weeks," he mutters, staring into my eyes. "Because all I think about is *you*. Every time I've touched you or kissed you or felt myself inside you? That was *real*. It was me needing to be close to you. Just like every *single* time I thought about you since you turned up on my balcony," he whispers, stroking my cheek.

He steps closer to me, only this time, I don't move away. He slowly reaches out and takes my hand, pulling me toward him. His lips press against mine. I whimper as I kiss him back. His fingers cradle my face as his mouth engulfs mine. He pulls away, long enough to stare into my eyes, and then he takes my hand, entwining his fingers around mine.

"Let's go for a walk," he murmurs.

"What about your dinner?" I say.

"I don't care about that. I'm not here because I want to be. I *have* to be here. Because he has no one else. I couldn't let him get up there and marry someone with no family at all on his side."

"You really love your brother, don't you?" I ask, smiling softly at him.

He nods and presses his lips together.

"When my parents died, I promised myself and Josh that I'd look after him. And now I can't seem to let go of that promise. Even though he's old enough now to look after himself, I still see him as my little brother. I feel this sense of obligation to him that I can't shake," he mutters, lowering his head.

We sit down on the edge of the river by the water. I snuggle against him as he wraps his arms around me and then kisses me on the forehead.

"What happened after they died?" I ask softly.

"We had an aunt that we didn't really know. She took us in. She was fine, but it wasn't really the same you know. We didn't get that same level of support and love that we got from our parents." He smiles sadly at me. "How close are you to your parents?"

"Very close to my dad," I say. "My mother died when I was little. My father has done his best to compensate for that, and honestly, he's done an amazing job, but that void is always there, you know?"

He nods. "Yeah, I know what you mean."

I hesitate. He's been so open with me that I feel like I need to do the same.

"I'm sorry if I overreacted earlier," I say. "It's just that I've been hurt before, and it's hard not to jump to the wrong conclusion."

"What happened?" he asks, frowning at me.

"I found him in bed with my best friend," I say. I laugh and shake my head. "I felt so stupid for not seeing the signs. I kept going over and over it in my head..."

"I'm sorry you had to go through that," he says earnestly.

We sit quietly for a few moments, until Chase stands. He puts out his hand and I place mine in his, laughing as I stumble into his embrace. He chuckles and kisses me.

"How would you like to go back to the hotel?" he asks. I

shiver, letting him wrap his arms around my shoulders to keep me warm.

"I'd like that."

WE WALK down the hallway toward our rooms, and he stops outside his and turns to me.

"I won't be offended if you want to go next door," he says, tracing his finger along my face.

I shake my head, and he smiles. He opens the door and leads me inside, pulling me back into his arms. I reach up and kiss him, pressing my lips against his. He groans as my hand travels down and over his erection.

My heart races as I reach for the buckle on his pants. I unbutton them and tug them down. He shrugs them off, kicking them out of the way, and then he practically rips the shirt clean off his chest.

"Very hot," I grin, admiring what I'm seeing.

"Your turn," he says as he steps closer to me.

He reaches behind my back to lower the zipper on my dress. It practically falls off me, pooling in a heap on the floor. I move it aside, then let him lead me by the hand across the room. He sits down on the bed, pulling me up against him. I lean over him, kissing him on the mouth as my hair falls around us. He lies back, taking me with him, expertly maneuvering us both up the bed until his head rests on the pillow. I straddle him as his hands roam over my stomach, while I gently grind myself against him.

"You amaze me," he mutters, shaking his head. "You can't even imagine what I was thinking when I saw you on my balcony."

I chuckle, heat creeping onto my cheeks. "I bet it wasn't nearly as dirty as what I *wanted* you to do to me," I say softly.

"Really? Then how about I show you?" he smirks.

He reaches up and lowers the strap of my bra, letting it fall over my shoulder. He does the same to the other side until my breasts are uncovered. I reach behind my back to unclasp it, and then toss it aside, still gently rocking against him. He looks down at my panties and runs his finger slowly over the material covering my pussy. I groan, my body aching for his touch.

"I was thinking very, *very* inappropriate things about you," he admits. "You have no idea how hard it was for me not to just carry you down to my bedroom and have my way with you. All I could think about was what you were hiding behind that tiny scrap of material covering your pussy."

Holy fucking hell.

I gasp as he lowers the band, just far enough to slide his tongue inside me, every part of me begging for more. He lifts me up and rolls my panties down over my thighs, then with one flick of his wrist, he tears them off me. I gasp as the material burns my skin.

"Better," he mutters, nodding his approval.

He guides me down onto his waiting cock. I moan softly as he penetrates me, his thick shaft sliding through my slick pussy with ease. With my hands firmly pressing onto his stomach, I ride him, loving the feel of him moving inside me.

He reaches up and grasps my breasts, pinching my nipples so hard that I gasp. He smirks, his hands moving everywhere. I groan as I rock myself harder against him, his cock delving deeper into me. My thighs clench. I groan and close my eyes, my pussy throbbing as I come.

"Oh God," I gasp, throwing my head back.

"God *yes*," he hisses, echoing me.

He closes his eyes and groans, thrusting forward as he releases inside me. I cry out as I come again, the second time more intense than the first. He growls and pumps his length into me as his grip on my hips tightens. With one final groan, he eases me off him and onto the bed next to him. I smile and kiss his forehead, through the thin film of sweat now covering him.

He breathes heavily, rolling onto his side and wrapping his arms around me. I sigh as he kisses my neck, loving the feel of his hot skin up against mine. I close my eyes and listen to the sound of his heart beating, while he wraps his arms protectively around me. I close my eyes, fighting the urge to fall asleep, until I can't fight any longer.

I ROUSE AGAIN, cracking my eyes open. It's morning, and the knocking on the door starts up again, reminding me that it was the reason I woke up in the first place. I roll over and glance at Chase, as he looks around, wide-eyed and still half asleep. I chuckle, because he looks more confused and disorientated than me.

"Someone's at the door," I whisper, sitting up.

He mumbles something under his breath as he climbs out of the bed and reaches for his pants. He throws them on, along with his shirt, quickly buttoning it up.

Yawning, he walks over and opens the door just enough, so that they can't see me still in bed. I listen, ashamed that I need to know what's going on, but not embarrassed enough to actually stop. It's a female voice, but I can't quite make out who it is. Then the talking stops and Chase glances back at me. One look at his face and I know who it is.

"It's Casey," he says, confirming my fears. "She wants to have a word with me. Would you mind..." He hesitates, so I make it easy for him.

"Sure," I say, way too brightly.

I get up, taking the sheet with me, and then disappear into the room next door before Chase can say anything else to me. I walk over to the bed and lie down, still wrapped in sheets that smell like him.

My heart pounds, because the guy I'm *pretty* sure I've falling in love with is in the room next to me, smelling of me whilst talking to his ex-wife. If that's not messed up, then I don't know what is.

But I've got nothing to worry about, right?

CHAPTER SIXTEEN
CHASE

"SO...CAN I COME IN?" Casey asks coyly.

She cocks her head and smiles at me. It's a look that used to work on me, but it doesn't anymore. I shrug and step aside, letting her into the room. I close the door and then turn around. I frown at her, not sure why she's here or what she expects me to say. She stares at me for a long time, before she looks away, like she's embarrassed.

And so she should be.

"Look, I just wanted to thank you," she says.

"For what?" I ask with a frown.

"For the last night? You were so nice and friendly with everyone...including me. I know that must have been hard," she says, looking up at me. "I know how much having you here means to Josh. I also know it's probably the *last* place you want to be." She pauses for a moment. "It's good to see you, Chase. You look happy."

"I guess I am," I say.

"Alana seems nice," she offers.

I nod and smile, my heart racing at the mention of her name. All I can think about is getting back to her and feeling the touch of her lips against mine. I could lock myself away with her for days, and it still wouldn't be enough.

"She's pretty special," I agree.

"If it means anything at all to you, I'm glad you've found someone who makes you happy," Casey whispers.

"Because that lessens your guilt?" I ask. Her face goes red, and I sigh.

I didn't need to say that.

"I'm not here to make you feel bad, Casey. I really am here for Josh. I didn't want him standing up there alone on a day that should be celebrated with family..."

I frown, realizing just how much we really need each other for support. We've missed out on so much over the past year because of this.

Casey shakes her head, tears filling her eyes.

"I'm sorry, Chase. I shouldn't have come here. I'm the last person you probably want to speak to, which I totally understand. It's just you were so friendly the other night that I thought we could get past this..." She shakes her head. "I'll see myself out," she mumbles.

I watch her as she walks over to the door. It never entered my mind to stop her, because she's right. She *is* the last person I want to be spending my time with right now. Just as she turns the handle to walk out, she turns back to me.

"One more thing," she says softly.

"Yes?" I say. I clench my hands into fists in my pockets. She can't look me in the eyes, so I know where this is going.

"I never did thank you. For not telling Josh the truth about what happened," she says.

"I love my brother," I reply, as if it's that simple. "It would have achieved nothing, other than him feeling as hurt as I was."

Her face falls. She nods and then walks out of the room.

I wait until she closes the door before I let myself relax. I sigh, my heart racing. I needed that, probably as much as she did, because things never really felt resolved between us. I hadn't realized how nervous I'd be about seeing her again until she was there in front of me the other night.

Today, even though not much was said, being able to look her in the eye and not feel like I was going to fall apart feels like a huge step forward. It's taken a year, but that chapter of my life has finally come to an end. I walk around the room for a moment to gather my thoughts. I flex my fingers, trying to get my blood flowing. My hands are shaking from the adrenaline still pumping through my body.

The only person I really care about, aside from my brother, is sitting in a room next to this one, no doubt wondering what the hell is going on. All the truth is doing right now is sitting in the back of my mind, festering away, while I worry how she's going to react when she finds out.

I need to tell her everything. If I don't, I'm going to lose her.

I walk over to the door connecting our rooms and gently knock, before opening it. She stands next to the bed, throwing her things into her suitcase. She doesn't look up, instead putting extra anger into her packing.

She's taking this well.

"What are you doing?" I ask her.

She zips up the case and then yanks it off, before glaring at me.

"I'll be here for the damn wedding, if that's what you're worried about," she mumbles.

"I don't care about that. I care about where are you're going. Are you leaving?" I ask her.

She sighs, finally stopping long enough to meet my gaze.

"I'm requesting another room. One on a different level."

"Away from me, you mean," I say, feeling hurt. She shrugs. "Why?" I ask.

"Why?" she repeats. Her eyes flash. "You *fucked* me all night, Chase. Do you remember that? You made me come *four* times. And then this morning, your ex-wife knocks on the door and I'm whisked into the other room. How do you think that made me feel?" she whispers, tears forming in her eyes. She sinks down onto the bed, her expression helpless. "God, I hate you *so much* for how you make me feel. I can't do this anymore, Chase."

She laughs hysterically. I watch her, alarmed as the laughter turns into tears.

Has she finally lost it?

"Your name is so applicable," she giggles through her tears. "Because that's what I feel like I'm doing. *Chasing* you." I sit down next to her.

"Do you want to know what we spoke about in there?" I ask. She stiffens, not answering me. I continue anyway. "You. Pretty much the whole time she was in there, I was talking about you."

"Really?" she asks. She frowns at me. "Why was she there in the first place?"

"Because we ended things badly," I say honestly. "We both needed closure." I reach over, placing my hand on top of hers. She relents, letting me move her closer to me. "In case I haven't made it crystal clear how I feel about you?" I snake my arm around the back of her neck and bring her face closer to mine. "*This* is how I feel," I murmur softly, pressing my lips against hers.

She sighs and lies back on the bed, while I lie next to her. I kiss her, just enjoying the feel of her lips against mine. I harden as her fingers move over my crotch, and I release a groan.

"If we didn't have a wedding to get ready for right now, you know exactly what I'd be doing to you," I mutter. She laughs and then smiles at me, enjoying the fact that she winds me up so damn much.

After a quick shower, I change into my tuxedo.

Standing in front of the mirror, I button up my jacket while staring at my reflection. I frown, because I feel more like I'm attending a funeral than a wedding. Alana walks into the room. I catch a glimpse of her in the mirror, and I'm stunned. I turn around and take her in, unable to form words to tell her how amazing she looks.

"Is this okay?" she asks, running her hands down over the dress. She frowns as she examines my expression, my lack of response obviously making her insecure. I shake my head and clear my throat.

"I can't even *begin* to tell you how beautiful you look," I say hoarsely.

My heart pounds as I walk over to her. I take her hand and wrap it around my waist, pressing my lips against hers.

"How am I supposed to get through today, when you're standing meters away from me, in that dress?" I ask. "I'll be thinking dirty, dirty things about you the entire time."

She laughs, her cheeks flushing red.

"Not to ruin the moment or anything, but we'd better get moving or risk walking in there late," she points out.

She takes my hand. I hesitate, because I really want to tell her everything before the wedding. But she's right. We don't have time. Enough eyes will be on me today already, without giving people another reason to hate me because we're late.

WE TAKE the elevator down to the ground floor and make the short walk across the hotel grounds to the little chapel down by the beach. Alana glances at me when we reach the doors, confusion in her eyes.

"If we're this close to the beach, why not get married on the beach?" she asks.

"Because Casey doesn't like sand," I smirk.

There's no one around==no one milling around outside, which means everyone is already inside, probably sitting down, waiting for those doors to open so they can all turn and stare at Casey. Only when they turn, they'll be getting an eyeful of me first.

"Are you ready?" she asks.

I nod. But then I laugh.

"Honestly? Not really, but I know that I need to do this. For Josh."

We walk inside, trying our best not to draw attention to ourselves, but it doesn't matter. I could've skydived in through the roof, wearing a tutu and nipple tassels, and it would've garnered the same reaction. Every pair of eyes in the chapel turns to stare at me. I feel sorry for poor Alana, because she's going to cop as much wrath I am.

I glance at her and she shrugs, like she can't understand their reaction. I can. But it's a hard thing to explain why everyone, including my own brother thinks that I cheated on my wife.

I hold my breath and smile as I see people I once knew, pretending I don't notice the disapproving glares and angry expressions. I expected a reaction, but this is extreme. *What were you expecting with a gathering of Casey's extended family and friends? A hug and a cheer?* I can't understand why Josh wanted me here at *all*, let alone to be his best man.

I leave Alana down by the door—which will come in handy if things get hairy and she needs a quick escape—and walk up to stand on the stage next to my brother. He glances over and squeezes my arm.

"Thanks for being here," he mumbles. Then he laughs. "Holy shit, I'm nervous. Is that normal? Were you this nervous when you..." His voice trails off. He stares at his feet, flustered. I smirk and choke back a laugh over what he was about to ask me. "Sorry man," he mutters, shaking his head. "I'm just not thinking straight at the moment."

"It's fine." I grin. "And yes I *was* this nervous when I married your wife."

The music starts playing. I straighten up a little and glance toward the door, along with everyone else in the room. They swing open and Casey appears. She looks stunning, as I expected, wearing an elegant, yet simple white dress.

She passes me on her way to Josh. I smile at her and she smiles back. I take a deep breath and clasp my hands in front of me as the celebrant begins the ceremony.

After they exchange their vows, and her mother reads a poem, the ceremony is concluded with their first kiss. I clap along with everyone else and smile at all the right times. Just when I think I can't take anymore, I glance down at Alana and see her watching me. She nods and blows me a kiss. I smile and look down, her belief in me enough to help me push on.

AFTER THE CEREMONY IS OVER, I walk back down to the front of the chapel, where Alana is waiting for me. I take her hand and squeeze it. As much I hate to admit it, I'm glad I was there to witness their marriage. I would have regretted it if I hadn't come.

"Glad that's over with?" she asks with a grin.

"More than you know," I murmur.

We walk outside and hang around until I'm done with the obligatory photos that I need to be present for, and then we're free for a couple of hours to do our own thing. Standing there with her family didn't feel awkward at *all*. The second I'm able to leave, I do, taking Alana's hand and leading her down to the river, where we sit down.

"What time does the reception start?" she asks.

"Four," I reply, glancing at my watch. "So, we have two hours to fill in."

"Two hours," she repeats slowly. She raises her eyebrows, her eyes sparkling. "How on earth are we going to manage that?"

I chuckle and stand up, taking her hand.

"I can think of a few ways," I tease. She giggles as she lets me help her to her feet.

WE RACE BACK to the hotel like a couple of horny teenagers, kissing and touching each other along the way. The moment the doors close on that elevator, I'm all over her. I tilt her face, so I can kiss her neck, and press her up against the wall. She groans as my hands roam over her dress. I press my mouth against hers.

She sighs, her hand running down over my erection. I

groan, barely able to control myself. At this point, I don't care *who* enters the elevator, because removing my hands from her body just isn't possible.

We stumble out on our floor and race down the hallway until we're outside our rooms. I lift her into my arms and swipe my key, swinging the door open, while still managing to kiss her. She sighs as I carry her over to the bed and throw her down. All I want to do is get her out of that dress and fuck her as hard as she can take it. She sits up, unzipping the back of her dress, while I watch. I step forward, ready to assist, but she stops me.

"Uh-uh. Stand back there," she says, a devilish smile forming on her lips.

I groan but do as I'm told.

She stands, ensuring that she's *just* out of my reach, before she lowers the delicate lace straps of her dress. I swallow, my throat dry as she inches the dress lower and lower, before eventually letting it go.

"Stay there," she murmurs, sensing my urge to touch her.

She reaches behind her back and unclasps her bra, holding the fabric over her breasts while she unthreads her arms. Then she slides her panties down over her legs, before stepping out of them.

God, she's incredible.

Fuck her rules. With a growl, I lunge forward and take her into my arms, throwing her back down on the bed. She laughs as I lift her legs over my shoulders. I unzip my pants and free my cock, lining it up with her pussy. She gasps as I thrust myself inside her with more urgency and determination than I ever have before. Watching her strip like that almost had me coming there and then, so I know I'm close.

I kiss her thighs as I ram myself into her. She gasps, reaching above her head to the wall for support. I growl as my body convulses, and I come, releasing hard into her wet pussy.

She gasps and clenches her thighs around my neck as my length fills her. Breathless and exhausted I groan as my movements slow to a gentle rock.

"Wow," she mumbles, her eyes wide. She laughs as I lower her legs and collapse onto the bed next to her. "Where the hell did that come from?"

"Sorry," I grin. "I guess seeing you in that dress really turned me on."

She smiles and rolls over, nestling into my arms. She falls asleep as I stroke her hair. I watch her, letting her rest, because she fucking earned it. When she wakes up, I'll tell her everything. I watch her sleep, in awe of how beautiful she is. The way she makes me feel is so surreal, like I can't quite let myself believe that things could be this good.

WE MAKE it back to the reception just before the bride and groom arrive. Even though I intended on staying awake, I must've fallen asleep, because the next thing I knew, it was nearly four.

We spend the next hour staying out of people's way and pretending that neither of us notice the whispering and pointing. *Maybe now would be a good time to tell her the truth.* I glance around to make sure we're alone, but before I can broach the subject, she turns to me.

"I'm just going to run to the bathroom," she whispers in my ear.

She'd been gone for a few minutes, when someone approaches me. They clear their throats, and I look up. I stiffen when I see Casey's parents standing there. I've done my best to avoid them all day, but it seems they were just waiting for the chance to talk to me alone. I haven't seen or spoken to them since before my split with Casey.

God knows what they think of me, or what she's told them.

"I guess I should thank you for not ruining our daughter's day," her father says gruffly.

"Oh, I did my best to refrain from doing that," I say.

I'm not helping the situation with my tone, but I can't help myself. I didn't even like them when Casey and I were together. He glares at me.

"You don't think it was a valid concern for us that you might pull some sort of stunt?" he leers. "You did ruin her life, after all."

I sigh and rub my head. I don't want to do this here, of all places, for Josh's sake, but if he keeps pushing me, I'm going to push back.

"I'm sorry for what happened between Casey and me—"

"Are you?" he barks, cutting in. "Because you seemed to have moved on. I'm so happy that you were able to move onto new things so quickly. Do you to have any idea how hard it was for Casey to get over you *cheating* on her?"

"Well, considering how quickly she jumped into my brother's bed, I'd say she got over me pretty damn fast," I retort.

I hear a gasp. I know it's Alana before I even turn around. She stands there, her eyes wide, staring at me.

"Shit," I mutter.

I knew there was a risk of her finding out like this, but I didn't expect it to be from my own mouth. She mutters something incoherent and then turns around, rushing out of the room.

"You better go after her, so you can ruin her life too," Casey's father chortles.

I glare at him, wanting nothing more than to wipe the smirk of his face—preferably with my fist, but I need to speak to Alana. I race outside and look around, spotting her running through the gardens, back toward the hotel.

"Alana, wait," I call out, but she doesn't stop.

I finally catch up to her just before she reaches the doors. I grab hold of her arm, stopping her in her tracks. She turns around and glares at me, the anger in her eyes making me step back. I thought all I needed to do was explain, and she'd understand, but now I'm not so sure.

"What?" she snaps. She wipes her glassy eyes.

"Just listen to me," I plead with her. "It's not as bad as it sounds—"

"Not as bad as it sounds?" she repeats with a laugh. "Jesus, Chase, am I stupid? Is that what you think when you look at me? It's *exactly* what it sounds like." She shakes her head. "You *bringing* me here in the first place is a joke. You've fed me one lie after another, and I've just sat there, guzzling them all up, like the fucking dickhead I am."

"Alana—"

"Don't. Just please, *don't.* I feel like enough of a fool already without you making this worse. Just leave me the hell alone, okay?" she whispers. "Go back to your warped little love triangle in there and leave me the fuck out of it."

"Not until you let me explain," I say, standing my ground.

"No," she shakes her head venomously. "You don't get to do this to me again, Chase. Even though you blindsided me into this whole mess, I *still* did my part. I pretended to be your girlfriend. Now, you *owe* me, so just leave me *alone.*"

She yanks her hand out of my grasp and runs inside, disappearing into the elevator. I stare after her, torn between giving her time to her calm down and chasing after her. *I should've just told her the whole truth in the first place.* The most fucked up thing is that what she *thinks* is the truth isn't even the half of it. Only Casey and I know the full story, but maybe it's time that changed.

I'll give her an hour to calm down and then try and talk to her again.

Forcing her to confront me isn't going to do either of us any good.

With one last look inside, I turn around and walk back over to the wedding. No matter how much I want to just crawl into a ball and drink myself to sleep, I need to plaster a smile on my face and pretend that I give a shit about any of this.

I can't abandon my brother.

An hour turns into two, and two turns into four, until I find myself creeping into my room at five in the morning. I'm very drunk, but that doesn't stop me from banging the hell out of the interconnecting door, demanding that she open up and listen to me. When she doesn't respond, I force my way through the door and into an empty room.

I stand there, my heart racing as I look around. All of her things are gone. I walk up to the bed and sink down on it. *Maybe she's just gone into another room.* But even as I think it, I know it's unlikely. *I shouldn't have let her leave like that.* I should've just come out and told her everything, right then and there. I owed her that much. With a groan, I lie back on the bed and close my eyes, the effects of the alcohol making my head spin like crazy.

I'll figure this out in a minute. I know there's a way for me to fix this; I just need to close my eyes for a second to work it out.

Pain shoots through my head, taking my breath away. I crack open my eyes. It's morning. I'm lying on Alana's bed, with my head crooked in an unnatural angle. Shit. I gasp as I straighten it, then somehow manage to roll over onto my stomach. I awkwardly stand up and rub my neck, trying to massage out the kink. I gasp, not sure if I'm helping it or making it worse. I stumble back into my room and pick up my phone.

Shit. I'm about to miss my plane. I frantically throw my things into my suitcase and zip it shut. I don't even bother changing, because I know I don't have the time.

After I check out, I flag down a cab to take me to the airport. My only saving grace is that traffic is minimal, so I arrived just as they're closing off the check-in booth.

"Please," I say after rushing up to the booth.

I'm out of breath and clearly a mess, so I hope she takes pity on me. When I think I almost have her, I flash her a smile. She almost visibly melts, her cheeks flushing.

"Okay, just this once, Mr. Winston," she says with a giggle.

Thank fucking God. It's good to know that even hungover and in desperate need of a shower, I've still got it.

I alternate the flight back between sleeping off my hangover and glancing longingly at the empty seat next to me. *Where is she right now?* She obviously caught an earlier flight—which she would've paid with using her own money, considering I had authorization over these two tickets. I think about what that means. I upset her so much that she couldn't stand being on the same flight as me.

I rub my head, trying to ease the aching. The worst thing is that I have no idea how to fix this mess. I tried calling her while waiting to board the plane, but she wouldn't answer, so I tried texting. Even if she *does* listen to me for long enough to hear me out, she's right. I still lied to her, *multiple* times. Would I forgive someone who'd lied to me more than they'd told the truth? Probably not.

I'm still hung-over and feeling sorry for myself when the flight lands, so I don't risk driving home. I call myself a cab and give the driver Alana's address. I don't intend on trying to speak to her, I just want to know she's safe. As we drive past her place, I can just make out the glow of a light inside. It doesn't make me feel much better, but not much will at this point. The driver looks at me and shrugs.

I guess I'll go home.

"Take me to four one one Wilson Boulevard instead, please," I order him gruffly.

I slump down in the seat and stare out the window. I hate not knowing where I stand. Okay, so I've got a pretty good idea of where I stand right *now*, but I hate not knowing if I can fix this. *God, I hope I can.*

I LAY in bed and stare at the ceiling, before my eyes dart to my phone again. I sigh when I see no texts or calls from her. I have no idea if she'll even be at work tomorrow. Not that that's high on my list of problems right now. I roll over and close my eyes, trying to will myself into sleeping, but it's no use. I can't get her out of my head. I just keep running over that moment, again and again.

In the end, I throw back the sheets and stalk out to the kitchen and reach for the bottle of scotch I keep on top of the fridge. I twist off the cap and gulp it down, not bothering with a glass.

Breathing hard, I lean against the counter. My hands run slowly over the surface as I remember how it felt to be inside her. Right here on this surface. It feels like so long ago. I hoist myself up and lie back, closing my eyes.

I GROAN AND shield my eyes from the sun that's pouring through the window. *Why the fuck am I out here?* I sit up, letting out a growl as my back sticks to the counter, practically ripping off a layer of skin.

Fuck me.

Jumping off the counter, I gingerly take a few steps. I spy the empty bottle of scotch lying beside the sink and sigh as bits of the night come back to me. All I wanted was to go to sleep and get her out of my head. *Fuck. Alana.* I glance around, looking for my phone. Alcohol and I are not a good mix when I'm depressed, so God only knows what kind of pitiful, desperate texts I sent her while inebriated or how many times I tried to call her.

I find my phone stuffed down the side of the couch. My heart pounds as I check the log first. *Five calls.* Not as bad as I was expecting. Then I check my text messages. *Twenty-Three?* Jesus, I'm surprised I got any sleep at all. I frown as I scroll through them.

Me: *Please just speak to me. Five minutes.*

Me: *Alana, please. Just hear me out.*

Me: *For fucks sake, I just want to talk...*

I stop reading, too nervous to see what the rest of them say. My head is pounding, and I think I feel worse than I did last night, if that's even possible. I sigh and toss my phone on the couch, catching sight of the time in the process.

"Fuck," I mutter.

It's nearly one in the afternoon and I should be at work. I have meetings all afternoon, including one with Phillip to discuss the Benson takeover bid that I want him to consider. As shitty as I feel, I refuse to let it affect my clients. I didn't get where I am today to fuck it all up over some girl.

But she isn't just some girl, is she?

The knock on the door stops me from entering an internal argument with myself. I walk over and open it, scowling at Josh. He smiles and follows me back inside, where I slump down on the couch.

"Well, you're a vision of happiness today," he comments.

"I'm not in the mood," I mutter.

"You're also not at work," he points out.

"Yeah? And how would you know that?" I realize the ridiculousness of my statement the second it leaves my mouth.

He chuckles. "What's up with you?"

I sigh. "It's nothing."

"Does this nothing have anything to do with Alana?" he asks gently.

I shrug. He sighs and sits forward.

"Whatever it is, fix it. She's good for you," he says.

"You don't think I know that?" I say with a snarl.

"Have you tried talking to her? Maybe if—"

"What, Josh?" I growl. "Maybe she'll forgive me? I can't even get her to hear me out." I sigh and rock forward on my feet. "Just stay out of it. I appreciate that you care so much, but you don't know what your fucking talking about."

I get to my feet and frown at him.

"Can you see yourself out? I have to get ready for work."

I stalk into my bedroom and slam the door shut without waiting for him to answer. Stripping out of my boxers, I run the shower in my bathroom, waiting for the water to run hot before I step in. I hear the sound of the front door closing, and I sigh, not feeling the relief that I thought I would. I lean against the tiles, angry at myself, angry at the world. I never should've let Casey blame me in the first place.

Why do I always have to fuck everything up?

CHAPTER SEVENTEEN
ALANA

"YOU'RE NOT GOING in today either?" Peyton asks. "I get that you're avoiding him, but why?" she asks. "Talk to me."

"I didn't *call* you for a heart-to-heart," I say with a growl. "Just call in sick for me again. *Please*," I add for effect.

"Only if you talk to me," she replies stubbornly.

"Fine," I mutter, not caring anymore. "If you want me to talk, then call in sick yourself and come over."

I hang up on her before she can respond, then I shove my pillow back over my head and attempt to go back to sleep. It works until, twenty minutes later, when someone pounds on my door.

"Let me in, Lanna!" Peyton's muffled voice floats through to my bedroom.

I groan because I didn't expect her to actually come over here. Reluctantly, I force myself out of bed and walk over to the door. I open it and frown at her. She ignores my pissed off expression and hands me a coffee. I take a sip as she guides me over to the couch and sits me down.

I got back late Sunday night after booking myself an earlier flight. I couldn't stand the thought of being that close to him for three hours, so I paid an obscene amount for a business-class ticket. Monday morning rolled around and the idea of seeing him still made me feel like hurling, so I called Pey. She didn't ask questions, but she knew something was up.

Today though, she *is* asking questions. I know I'm not going to get away with not telling her everything. Who knows, maybe talking about it is exactly what I need? Maybe if I get it all out, I'll feel better and be able to put this behind me and move on.

"Now, tell me what the hell happened," she says. "Don't try and tell me it's a coincidence that Chase didn't turn up until three in the afternoon yesterday, either."

I release a big sigh and lie back on the couch, closing my eyes, hating that hearing that makes me feel good. Where do I even begin to try and explain this to her?

"He lied to me," I say, then I laugh, because that doesn't even *begin* to cover it. "Well, really, it was lie after lie after fucking *lie*. I think I'm pretty understanding, but even I have limits."

"What did he do?" she asks.

"I told you that the big meeting he needed me there was to see his brother marry his ex-wife," I begin. She nods and takes my hand. "I found out the reason they split up. Chase *cheated* on her." I shake my head, all the anger and emotions feeling as raw as it did yesterday. "I sure know how to pick them, don't I?"

Peyton shakes her head. "Oh, honey. I can't believe that he'd *do* something like that. Are you sure it isn't just someone trying to cause trouble for him?"

"I heard him say the words himself. He was talking to her parents and I overheard." I twirl my cup around the palm of my hands. "Jesus, Pey. I mean, what's to stop him from doing it again and cheating on me?" I ask with a frown. I blink back tears, because it all feels too real. "I can't go through that again. I promised myself that I'd never let anyone treat me like that again," I say. I shake my head and laugh as I look at her. "Am I making a bigger deal out of this than it needs to be?"

She gets up, stepping over to the couch to where I am. She sits down and wraps her arms around me, kissing me on the cheek.

"No, you're not. You did the right thing, getting out of this before things went any further. I know it hurts, but it's better finding this out now than after you've fallen in love with him," she adds, wiping away my tears.

"I think it's too late for that," I mumble as she strokes my hair, soothing me.

"I can stay if you need me to," she says. "I told them I was running late, but I can say that I won't be in at all."

"No." I frown. "I'm not very good company right now, and it would be just my luck that he'd fire you because of it. If you call in sick, he'll totally know that you're here with me."

She nods and kisses me on the cheek.

"I hate leaving you like this." She frowns. "Call me if you need me, and I'll stop by on my way home too."

"Thanks, Pey," I say, giving her a squeeze.

After I walk her out, I have a shower in an attempt to try and feel at least a little bit human. I feel marginally better, but not enough to actually motivate myself into getting up and doing anything. Instead, I lay in my bed and try to distract myself with a book. The problem is, all I can manage is a few pages before my mind replays what he said to her parents.

God, I'm so angry at him.

All the messages and phone calls in the world won't make me listen to him right now. He lied right to my face. I bet he doesn't even feel bad about it. He got what he needed from me, after all. I can't believe I actually fell for all of the bullshit he fed me. Am I that naïve?

I click out of my Kindle and bring his number up. My finger hovers over his name, my heart pounding. I just want to let him know how I feel, but I can't do it. Frustrated, I toss the phone across the bed, just as someone knocks on the door.

Peyton. She'll be impressed that I'm dressed.

I climb off the bed and walk over, peering through the people before I open it. *Shit.* It's not Peyton at all. It's Chase's brother.

Josh stands there, looking around as he shifts from foot to foot. He looks nervous. *Why is he here?* Did Chase send him to try and talk to me? I'm tempted to pretend that I'm not home, but my curiosity gets the best of me.

I open the door and frown at him.

"Hey," he says flushing an embarrassed smile. "Sorry to turn up like this..." He hesitates. "I was hoping that I could talk to you."

"About what, exactly?" I say, my tone guarded. "And how did you know where I live?"

"I, uh, found it in my brother's phone while he was in the shower," he murmurs with a wince. "Look, I'm not here to cause you any trouble. I just wanted you to know that Chase is seriously cut up about whatever went wrong between you two. I haven't seen him this worked up about anyone since..." His voice trails off.

"Since Casey," I say flatly. He nods. "I appreciate you coming over here, but it was pointless. He cheated on Casey. I know that it wasn't me, but I've been hurt before by someone I thought that I could trust, and I can't go through that again."

Why am I even saying all of this? I don't owe anyone an explanation, least of all him.

"Give me five minutes," he pleads, a look of pain passing through his eyes.

I sigh and nod for him to come in. He points at the couch and motions for me to sit down. I sigh, but I do as he asks and sit, my hands clasped in front of me, waiting for his big piece of news that will change everything.

"He didn't cheat on Casey, Alana."

I stare at him. "What?" I say, frowning. *Now he's lying too?* Maybe it runs in the fucking family.

"It didn't happen like that." He sighs and sits back in the

chair, running both hands through his hair. "I'm sorry, but this is really hard for me to say."

"Take your time," I say, not sure what's going on.

He nods. "Their marriage wasn't a good one. Chase had one focus: his career. Casey struggled with not being put first in their relationship. He was working a lot and she couldn't handle that. She felt unloved and unwanted. A professor started paying attention to her. She rejected his advances, but after a while, she started to let things happen. That fling ended very badly one night. Naturally, she couldn't speak to Chase about it, so she called me."

"She cheated first?" I mumble. He looks up at me, his eyes meeting mine.

"She was the *only* one who cheated, Alana." He rubs his eyes and sighs. "I knew they were having issues, but I had no idea how bad things were. When I picked her up, I knew something major had happened. She panicked and told me that Chase had been cheating on her and that she'd caught him. She didn't know what to do. She was so upset, and I was so angry at my brother for treating her like that." He presses his lips together, still torn up over it. "Focusing on his career was one thing, but to turn to other women, when he had an amazing one at home waiting for him every night? That wasn't right."

"So, did you confront Chase?" I ask. I can't believe what I'm hearing. "I don't understand how she could get away with saying it was him. I mean, surely the first thing you would do is confront him?"

"I wanted to, but she begged me not to. She asked me to

stay, because she didn't want to be alone, and..." He stops, looking down at his hands. "I did something I'll always regret that night. I told myself so many times that it was justified, because he *cheated* on her, but even if that were true, it would still be wrong."

"Then what happened?" I ask softly. My heart races, thinking about how Chase must have felt when he found out.

He shrugs. "Casey kept calling me. I was the only person she could talk to. We grew closer, and I eventually realized that I was in love with her." He groans and shakes his head. "The first thing Chase knew about *any* of this was when he caught us. The same night Casey asked him for a divorce. I'll never forget the look in his eyes when he saw us like that. There was no anger or hate. It was worse than that. He was disappointed in me."

"He caught you?" I whisper. *Oh God.* "Did he confront you or ask you why?" I mumble, my heart breaking for him.

"I think he was expecting it. Not *us*, but he knew she wasn't happy. I hated that he could make *me* feel guilty when *he* was the one who wronged her, and I went crazy at him over it. I wanted answers. I asked him how he could cheat on her. He looked me in the eye and he shrugged."

Josh raises his eyes to mine.

"Sometimes you hurt the people you love, even though you don't mean it. That's what he said to me," he mutters. "All along, it was *me* hurting *him*."

"How did you find out?" I whisper. I feel for the guy. God, I feel for *both* of them.

He laughs bitterly. "Believe it or not, Casey told me. She chose our wedding night to sit me down and tell me that she had been the one who'd cheated." Josh shakes his head, angry. "You have no idea how it feels to discover that you've betrayed your own brother. And he did *nothing* about it. God, he stood there by my side and watched me marry the woman who fucking ruined his life. How am I supposed to live with myself after that?"

I shake my head, wishing that I had answers for him.

"I just don't get why," I say softly. "*Why* would he take the rap for it?"

Josh shrugs. "I guess he could see how happy I was. He knew how guilty I'd feel if I knew that she was the one who cheated, and *I* was one of the people she'd cheated with."

He sits forward, and then he straightens himself up, meeting my eyes.

"Look. I'm not here for your pity or to make you feel bad. I just thought you should know the kind of man my brother really is and decide what you want to do based on the truth, rather than just half of it."

He stands and walks over to the door. I follow him, still not sure what I'm supposed to do now.

"Will you be okay?" I ask him suddenly. I can't imagine what he's going through. To find all of this out on your wedding night? I shudder, feeling for the poor guy.

"I don't know," he mumbles. "Ask me in a few weeks?"

"You said you came here to tell me the truth," I say, something hitting me. "How did you know that I knew?"

He smiles. "Casey. She saw the exchange between Chase and her parents. I think your reaction is what prompted her to be honest with me."

Wow. I wasn't expecting that.

I watch him leave, not sure how I'm feeling, other than lost and a barrage of other emotions that are doing nothing for helping me decide on what to do next.

I need to talk to Chase. I need to hear all of this from him.

Because that's the only way I'm going to know what the truth really is.

CHAPTER EIGHTEEN
CHASE

"AND DON'T BOTHER COMING BACK in tomorrow," I growl.

I slam down the phone and rest my head on my desk. Despite what people may think, I don't like firing people, but when they've proven themselves to be incompetent, unreliable fuckwits, what other choice do I have?

As it turns out, I've encountered a lot of them these last few days. It's completely coincidental that it coincides with me still not hearing from Alana. All I want is a chance to explain things from my point of view. If she just took two seconds to hear me out, she'd realize that things are not quite what they seem.

"God, Alana, what are you doing to me?" I mutter.

I MANAGE to get through to the end of the day without calling her again, but when I leave the office, I find myself driving past her place. I've done the same thing every night since we got back. I even worked up the courage to knock on her door last night, but she wouldn't answer. I don't know if she was in there or not. Either way, it didn't matter, because I left feeling just as worked up as I was when I got there.

Today when I pull up outside her building, I sit there in my car, trying to figure out all the things I want to say to her. *I should write her a letter and slide it under her door.* No. This is the kind of thing I need to say to her in person. I can't just come out and tell her the truth, because it's been hidden inside me for so long that it feels like part of me.

Not only that, if Josh found out the truth and it wasn't from me, I'm not sure how he would react. Not that I think for a second that she would go gossiping around town about me, but this affects more than just me.

I'm about to start my car and leave when I look up and see Josh.

My hands clench onto the steering wheel as I stare at him, sure I'm seeing things. Why is he leaving her place? I don't know what to think, so I let the irrational thoughts take over. *Is he doing it again?* First Casey, now Alana. It's a ridiculous thought but knowing that and believing it are two different things.

Instead of walking over there and asking him why he's there, I take the easy way out and leave. I'm way too wound up to talk to him like this. I take off down the street, my pulse racing out of control. I'm not sure where I'm going, but I just need to get out of her neighborhood. I drive randomly around the streets, my head a mess. All this anger isn't healthy. *I need to get to the root of the problem and deal with that if I have any chance of fixing this.* There's only one person I need to speak to in order to sort out what I'm feeling, so that's where I head.

I bang on her door for five minutes straight, before it swings open.

Casey stands there, staring at me, looking bewildered.

"Chase," she murmurs. "If you're here to see Josh, he's not home," she adds.

"I'm not here to see Josh," I say calmly. "I'm here to see you. Her eyes widen at the anger in my voice and to be honest, it's shocking even me. "Why?" I ask her. "I need to know why you did it."

She stares at me as if she doesn't know how to answer me. Tears well in her eyes, and for a second, I feel bad. And then I remember she was in the wrong. Not me.

"Chase, it was a long time ago—"

"Bullshit," I cut in. "It was barely two years ago. Josh was *sure* that I'd been cheating on you. That was his justification for doing what he did. He got that from somewhere, so I just need to know what you told him."

"I didn't tell him anything," she says quietly. "He assumed. And you didn't correct him? Isn't that just as bad?"

She doesn't answer. Her eyes dart around me.

"Look, can we not do this on my front doorstep?" she asks. Her lip trembles.

I nod stiffly and stalk past her into the living room, but I don't sit down. Sitting down would suggest I'm willing to make peace and compromise, and I have *no* intention of doing any of that. Not until she gives me the answers I need.

"I *loved* you. I was devoted to you and you left me for *him*?"

"Devoted?" she says with a laugh. "You were devoted to your *job*. You didn't care about me or appreciate me."

"That's not true," I growl. "Why do you think I worked so goddamned hard at my job? I wanted to give you security—"

"I didn't want security," she screams. "I wanted *you*. I wanted you to put me first. But you couldn't give me that. You couldn't let yourself be open enough to let me into your heart."

I stare at her, letting her words sink in. She's turning this all around on me? I shake my head.

"Where is Josh," I ask. I already know he's not here, but I want to know if she knows where he is.

She shrugs helplessly. "I don't know. I told him the truth," she says quietly.

My eyes widen. "What? When?"

"On our wedding night," she says quietly. She sits down. I sit opposite her, still in shock. I can't believe she actually told him.

"How did he take it?" I ask.

She laughs. "Not well. He looked at me the same way you're looking at me."

"I have to go," I mutter.

I stand up while she looks at me, her expression begging me to say something, but I have nothing. So, I just turn around and walk out the door and back over to my car.

I sit behind the wheel, feeling tense and angry. My head is

full of a hundred different thoughts. If Josh knows, then why did he go to see Alana? To fix my mess and tell her the truth? I frown, clutching the wheel tightly. He had no right doing that. His interference was only going to make this a thousand times worse.

I start driving, and before I know it, I've ended up at Lincoln Memorial Garden. I park my car in the street, and just sit there for a while, reflecting on the last time I was here.

It's been a long time. I think I was seventeen and only here because Josh had begged me to bring him. I struggled with visiting them here, and he respected that. He never pressured me to leave the car or ask me why I couldn't go and talk to them. I was so angry at them for so long and talking to them as though they were still alive felt silly. It didn't change anything. It didn't fix the way I felt inside, so why bother?

After Josh turned sixteen, he stopped asking me to come. It became so much easier to not visit when he didn't rely on me for it. And now, before I know it, nearly fifteen years has passed. Fifteen years. It feels surreal to think it was that long ago. What kind of son doesn't visit his parents' graves for over fifteen years?

Apparently, me.

I'm not sure why today is so different, but I get out of my car and walk through the gardens, over to where their ashes are scattered. I stand there, staring at the tree where their plaque sits, deep in thought.

Something Casey had said really stuck with me. Was she right? Did I not let her in? Was I incapable of loving anyone, in case they ended it? Did I keep people at a distance so I wouldn't end up getting hurt again?

I take a deep breath and walk a few meters over, so that I'm ironically enough of a distance away when I sit down. I stare at the ground, my stomach churning, because I don't know what to do. Where to go from here. I know I need to try and talk to Alana again, but the thought of doing that, especially now that she knows the truth, is hard. She'll have so many questions, like why did I let Josh believe all this time that I cheated on Casey? The hard thing is I can't even answer that question. I can tell that I didn't want him to get hurt all I like, but I know that it's more than that.

"I never thought I'd see you here." I stiffen and look up into my brother's eyes.

"What are you doing here?" I ask him gruffly. He shrugs and sits down next to me.

"Believe it or not, I come here a lot. It's a great place to think," he says. I nod and look down at the ground.

"Casey told me everything," he adds.

'I know, I've just come from her place," I mutter.

"Really, why?" he asks. I shrug, because I don't even know anymore.

"I should've told you the truth back then," I admit. "I thought I was doing the right thing in looking out for you."

"I know. I'm not angry at you, Chase. I know your heart was in the right place. I've known that since they died. You felt this need to look after me, and I'm sure that's what you thought you were doing by keeping this from me." He reaches over and wraps his arm around my shoulder.

"I went to see Alana."

"I know," I growl.

"Jesus, is there anything you don't know? How do you know?" he asks with a frown.

"Because I was sitting at the front of her place and I saw you leave."

"Why were you sitting there?" he asks shaking his head in confusion. "And if you got that far, why didn't you just go up and try and talk to her?"

"Don't you think I've tried that?" I bark at him, annoyed. "I do that a thousand times a day. I call her, send a text, I knock on her door; she doesn't want anything to do with me."

"So, you try again," Josh argues. "You're the one who taught me never to give up. Remember? You made me see that anything is possible if you believe in yourself. And now you're going back on that?" He sighs, taking a moment to compose himself. "Look. Do me a favor and give it one last chance. Go there and try and talk to her, because this time I'm confident that she'll listen to you."

"Because you told her the truth?" I frown.

"I *did* tell her," he admits. "But it wasn't to hurt you, Chase. I just know how stubborn you are. By the time you figured out she needed the truth, you'd have lost her."

"It wasn't your call to make," I mutter.

"Just like covering for Casey wasn't your call?" he asks gently. I flush. "I was angry at you at first, but then I realized you were just trying to protect me." He reaches over and pats me on the shoulder. "You've been carrying around my burden for too long. Let it go. Let me deal with this, okay?"

I nod and get to my feet. "Fine. I'll try and talk to her again, then." I turn and wait for Josh to get up, but he doesn't. Instead, he shakes his head and smiles at me.

"I think I'll stay here for a little while. I'll call you tomorrow, okay?"

After five minutes of relentless knocking on Alana's door, I sigh and turn around. I lean against the door, my hands shoved deep in my pockets. She's not there. Either that, or Josh was wrong, and she *is* in there, but she doesn't want to talk to me. I throw my hands up, frustrated. Either way, it doesn't matter, because I can't do this anymore, at least not tonight.

I drive home, trying to block all thoughts of her out of my head. When I exit the elevator on my floor, I stop in my tracks, because there she is, sitting at the front of my apartment. She looks up, her eyes widening, like I've caught her off guard. *Perhaps she was expecting more of a warning.* She gets to her feet.

"Can we talk?" she asks, her expression uncertain.

"That's all I've wanted for the last three days." I say with a frown.

"I know. I'm sorry," she says, her eyes glassy. She takes a deep breath and takes my hand. Then she laughs. "God, I had everything I wanted to say worked out in my head, and now it's all gone to shit."

"I'm the one who should be sorry, Alana," I murmur. I entwine her fingers around mine, my eyes not leaving hers. "I should've told you the truth from the beginning, as soon as we got to the wedding. The *whole* truth. Not just—"

She puts her finger to my lips, shutting me up.

"It's okay," she says. "I lied about something too."

"Oh?" I say, my heart racing.

She nods, a smile creeping across her lips. "When I said I wanted to talk, I really meant something else..."

I chuckle as she takes my hand and leads me into the bedroom.

Wrapping her arms around my neck, she kisses me on the lips. I groan as her fingers move down over my chest, her fingers frantically working to undo the buttons on my shirt. She frees the last one and then peels it off me, tossing it on the floor. With a raised eyebrow and a cheeky smirk, she moves down to my pants, unbuckling as she presses her lips against mine. I groan and shrug them off, along with my boxers.

She steps back. My gaze moves over her body, and I growl, wanting nothing more than to explore every inch of her beautiful, creamy skin. I shake my head and take her hand, pulling her into my arms.

"Ah," she cries out, laughing as I lay her over my shoulder and then toss her down on the bed. I climb on top of her, peeling her shirt off over her head. She lifts her ass, allowing me to roll her leggings down over her thighs.

I grunt as I stare at the sight in front of me. She lays on my bed, wearing only her bra and panties. I reach out and touch her toes, sliding my hands slowly up over her legs. I lower myself onto her, my lips finding her breasts. My heart races at the feel of her soft skin against my mouth. I push the cup of her bra down to reveal her breast, and then I close my mouth over the nipple.

She gasps, her back arching off the bed as I swirl my tongue around it, flicking it until it's stiffer than my cock. I move on to her other breast, sucking and flicking until it's also stiff. Then she rolls me over. I look up at her, surprised by her force and watch her as she peels off her panties. She gently rocks herself against me, her firm breasts bouncing as she lowers herself down onto my length. She gasps as I fill her, gently rocking against my rhythm.

I groan, struggling to contain myself as she slides down harder and faster onto me. I run my hand over her stomach and massage her breasts, pinching her nipples between my fingers. I growl, my heart racing as my orgasm begins to build. She gasps and cries out, closing her eyes as she contracts around my dick.

"Fuck," I groan, my cock throbbing as I release into her tight pussy.

Panting, she rolls off and snuggles into me, wrapping my arms around her. She wiggles closer, so her ass is against my cock, nuzzling against my hand. She gazes up at me and presses her lips softly against mine. She smiles as I kiss her.

"I'm glad you let me explain my side of things," I say with a grin.

She rolls over and props herself up on elbows.

"I should've let you explain what happened. I just panicked when I heard you say you cheated," she admits. "I told you I went through something with my boyfriend and best friend. That took me a long time to get over." I lean down and caress her face, angry that anyone would do that to her.

"I'll never treat you like that," I promise, kissing her on the nose. "And if you ask me, your ex-boyfriend is a total jerk and a fucking fool for doing that to you." She smiles and snuggles back against me, resting her head on my chest.

"You should take tomorrow off and make it up to me," she mumbles, her words barely coherent.

I chuckle and gently tickle her back as she sighs. Her breathing grows heavier as she drifts off to sleep. I kiss her forehead and just watch her for what feels like forever. I don't want to go to sleep because this moment is so perfect that I just want to last.

I nearly lost her once. I don't intend on letting myself fuck up like that again.

CHAPTER NINETEEN
ALANA

TO HIS CREDIT, he did take the day off—*six months later,* for our anniversary.

Well, at least the intention was there, until he was called in for a last-minute meeting. I frown at him as he hangs up the phone and rolls back over to face me. He winces when he sees my expression.

"Shit, I know. I promised. Someone else can handle it," he says, picking up the phone again. "You're more important than anything—"

I laugh and push him out of the bed. Honestly, I was surprised he even remembered the anniversary, because I sure as hell didn't.

"It's fine," I say with a laugh. "You can go into work for this meeting without upsetting me."

"I'll make it up to you," he promises.

"By handing me your credit card so I can entertain myself shopping?" I ask sweetly.

He rolls his eyes. "Since when do you even ask for it anymore?"

I think about going shopping. I'm sure that there's a lot I can buy with this platinum credit card, but in the end, I'm too lazy and spend most of the day napping around his pool. That is, until he interrupts my sunbathing at around two in the afternoon with a phone call.

"Can you come in for a little while?" he asks.

I frown. "I thought I had the day off?"

"You do," he says, "but Peyton is sick and I'm way behind. I have a big meeting that I need—"

"Calm down, I'll come in," I say as I roll my eyes. "But you so you owe me for this."

I get change into my work clothes and grab my keys and then make my way downstairs to my hail a cab. In the end, I decide to walk. It's not that far from his place, and me being a few minutes late isn't going to kill him. If he'd promoted me already like we agreed, then he'd have another assistant there, ready to kiss his ass. *Hold on. I'm not sure I like that idea.*

Every time I broach the subject of my internship, he promises me it's happening soon. First, it was waiting until the latest mergers were settled before introducing me to the team, but then, we were so close to the next quarter that he wanted to wait until then. I trust him that it's coming, but if it doesn't happen soon, I might have to withhold sex. I chuckle. *That will speed things up.*

I walk toward Chase's office, I run into Peyton. I frown at her.

"What's wrong?" she asks, her eyes wide.

"Nothing," I mumble, confused. "It's just that Chase asked me to come in because he was snowed under because *you'd* called in sick."

She laughs, looking at me like I'm crazy. "What? I haven't called in sick all year. Come find me when you speak to him though, okay? I have to get this to the mailroom or he'll have a stroke." She rolls her eyes and rushes off, still laughing as she disappears down the hallway.

I shake my head and walk through my small office, to Chase's door, knocking gently on it. He calls out for me to come in, so I do.

"What is this about? I thought you said that Peyton..."

My voice trails off when I see Philip sitting on the other side of Chase's desk. They both stand up and smile at me.

"Hi," I say, feeling flustered.

What the hell is this all about?

Chase motions for me to sit down. I walk over and sit next to Phillip. I glare at Chase, because I hate being blindsided. He knows *that* better than anyone. I have no idea what's going on, and if I don't find out soon, I'm going to snap.

"Philip asked me to get you in here," he says.

Well that confuses the hell out of me. Why would he want to see me?

He motions for Phillip to talk, who nods and turns to me.

"Chase came to me a few months ago with an interesting

proposal. At first, I was ready to laugh him out of the room, but then I decided to hear him out. By the end of it, I was ready to take a chance on a company that was struggling and would appear to have nothing to offer." He pauses and glances back at Chase.

"I'm not sure if you know that we closed that deal two months ago."

I glance at Chase. "Why didn't you tell me that?" I frown.

"Hear Phillip out," he asks me.

I turn back to Phillip, who continues.

"We redeveloped their entire marketing strategy, their manufacturing process and their management. We thought about what we should be highlighting about the product and went with it. Everything was overhauled, except for the product. Last month, that product alone produced one of our biggest profit months in our history."

"When I told Phillip the takeover was your idea, he didn't believe me," Chase adds.

Phillip nods. "I struggled to see potential in that company, so I couldn't see how someone with little experience in this field could. I've been looking into you, Alana. I know you graduated college majoring in statistics in business, and you have been working here ever since, right?"

"That's right," I say.

"What do you want to do?" he asks.

I glance at Chase. "Well, I want to work for the analytics department here—"

"Such a waste," he cuts in, shaking his head. "I want to offer you a job with my company."

"You want me to work for you?" I ask, shocked. I glance at Chase.

"No, not for me, with me," Phillip corrects. "I'm offering to mentor you, Alana. Show you everything I know."

"I don't know what to say," I reply, too stunned to think of anything else. I glance at Chase, who smiles at me.

"You can start with yes," Phillip laughs.

"It's an amazing opportunity. I wouldn't be hesitating to say yes," Chase agrees.

"I guess there is only one thing for me to say, then," I grin. "Yes."

"Fantastic. Call my assistant and arrange a meeting so we can go over the final details." He nods. "Chase, I'll leave you to it." I wait until Philip has left the room before I run around and throw my arms around Chase's neck. He laughs as I kiss him.

"Did you have anything at all to do with that?" I ask narrowing my eyes at him. He shakes his head.

"I wish I could take credit for it, but no. Do you have any idea how hard it is to get a job with that man?"

I shake my head, still feeling overwhelmed.

"That would mean leaving here," I say, sitting down on his desk.

"With what I can teach you, compared to what you can learn working for him, it's not even a decision," he says. "You're taking the job, even if I have to fire you to do it."

"But how will you cope without me here?" I ask with a frown.

"The man who's gonna fuck up my coffee, time and time again, he smokes us all," I say sticking my tongue out at him.

"Hey," I ask, grinning. "You'll be looking for a new executive assistant, right?"

Chase frowns at me. "Yes, why?"

I RACE out of the room and straight over to Peyton to share my good news. "That's amazing," she gushes, throwing her arms around me.

Chase sticks his head in the door.

"Peyton can I speak to for a moment?" he asks.

She stares at me, her eyes wide. I shrug and play innocent, but I know exactly what he's doing, and if anyone deserves this, it's her.

I leave the office calling Dad on my way home. He's happy to hear that I'm finally moving on away from what he still considers a hostile work environment.

"You do remember that he's my boyfriend, right?" I ask with a laugh.

"Right," he says, sounding embarrassed. "I guess I should think before I speak, huh? How long have you two been together now?"

"Six months today." I say, my smile widening.

"I'm proud of you," he says, "and glad you're happy. That's the most important thing to me."

"Hey, maybe we can double date?" I burst out laughing.

"What! I've been trying to find a way to tell you about Macy."

"Macy..." I say with a grin, "She sounds cute."

"She is that," he says sounding flustered. "We've been seeing each other for two months now."

"You've been holding out on me!" I say with a laugh. "Is this the same woman you were trying to tell me about nearly six months ago?"

"What?" he gasps. "You knew what I wanted to talk to you about? Why didn't you say something and put me out of my misery?"

"Because I figured you'd tell me when you were ready."

"No, that was June. She fizzled out after a few weeks. Macy though, she's a keeper."

I laugh. "Poor June."

"Yeah, yeah. Just call me to arrange dinner, okay? I want you to meet her. Now, go out and celebrate or something. Make that boyfriend of yours buy you dinner."

"I will," I say, with a giggle.

I hang up, then decide, what the hell, I *will* go shopping. I want to buy myself something nice, but after a foot massage and a day at the spa getting my nails done, I'm exhausted, and all I want to do is get home to Chase.

As I WALK BACK through the mall toward my car, I see Jade. I duck behind a row of jackets, so she doesn't see me. I cringe.

What am I doing? Surely, I can say hello to her without diving for cover? Just as I'm about to approach her, I see her slip a scarf into her handbag and walk off. I stare, wide-eyed, shocked at what I've just witnessed.

I'm still thinking about Jade when I arrive back at Chase's apartment, but that's soon forgotten when I walk in and find him preparing dinner. I put my bag down on the hall table and wander into the kitchen, wrapping my arms around his waist. I kiss the back of his head and then sit down on one of the stools on the other side.

"You're home early," I say with a grin.

He shrugs. "I told you, I was only going in for that meeting." He sets down his wooden spoon and wanders around the counter and kisses me roughly on the mouth. His brow creases. He leans closer again and breathes in deeply.

"You smell...floral."

"I had a massage," I say, casually handing back his credit card, my cheeks glowing, "Thanks for that. *Oh.* You'll never guess who I saw shoplifting today."

"Who?" he asks, soundly mildly interested.

"Jade," I grin.

He raises his eyebrows. "As in Jade who used to work for me?"

I nod. "I still can't believe you fired her to get closer to me."

He chuckles. "Is that what you thought? I fired Jade because she was stealing from my company. I'd been noticing the books weren't balancing for a while, but I didn't have any proof until I saw the sheets for that month."

"Oh," I say, flushing.

"But I think it's cute that you thought that." He raises his eyebrows. "So, I guess I'm not shocked by the shoplifting. And while I'm glad you enjoyed your massage, I already got you a present."

"Really?" I say raising my eyebrows.

He walks back over to the stove to stir his sauce, then wanders into the living room to retrieve a small, flat box.

I take the box from him and open it, pulling aside the white tissue paper to reveal a red lace, *very* sexy bra and matching thong. I stare at him, my mouth hanging open. He laughs at my reaction.

"I was thinking," he murmurs, his eyes twinkling as he pulls me into his arms. "That we could recreate that time when you tried to break in here?"

"I wasn't trying to break in," I scoff.

"Fine, whatever." He smirks. "Now let me help you put this on so you can get that ass of yours outside."

I STAND on the balcony wearing the sexy, red underwear, tapping on the window. I laugh, because I can't believe I'm doing this. Didn't I learn from the first time? He finally slides open the door...wearing no shirt. *Okay, so maybe this isn't all bad...*

"Hey," he says, looking me up and down. My heart races as he leans closer to me.

"Hey," I say back, biting back a smirk.

He takes my arms and pulls me inside, kissing his way along my neck. He lowers the straps on my bra, his tongue sliding along my collarbone. He reaches behind my back to unclasp my bra. Then he stops. He frowns, his brow creasing.

"What's this?" he asks, pulling his hand back.

"What..." I stare at him, my gaze dropping to the massive princess cut diamond he's holding in his hand.

"No," I say, shaking my head. He nods.

"Will you marry me?"

"Yes," I whisper, throwing my arms around him. "God, I love you." I kiss him on the lips and then hug him again, tears welling in my eyes.

"I love you, too," he says, his voice serious. Then he chuckles, a cheeky gleam flashing in his eyes.

"What?" I say suspiciously.

"Nothing. I was just thinking how much you're going to blush when everyone asks you to describe the moment when I proposed." He chuckles.

"You're an *asshole*," I say with a gasp. I step back and narrow my eyes at him. "You planned that, didn't you?" I accuse him.

He kisses me and takes my hand, leading me inside the bedroom.

"You fucking bet I did."

ABOUT TOO MUCH INFORMATION

We've all been there.

One minute, you're sprawled out on your bed, minding our own business and the next you're lying in the back seat of your best friend's car as she races you to the ER.

And not the closest one either.

No. You're headed to the one fifty miles farther out, because the one five minutes away is where you start your residency next week.

So there you are, lying in cubicle nine, hoping like hell that the doctor about to examine you isn't young, sexy or male.

Of course he's all three.

Telling him about the clitmaster7000 I have lodged inside me is by far the single most embarrassing moment of my life.

Discovering he's my brother's new roommate is even worse.

Keep reading for a sneak peek!

TOO MUCH INFORMATION EXCERPT

LAURA

I take a deep breath and glance at the courier email again. It's well past their allotted "four hour" time frame, and I've got better things to do than stand around my apartment waiting all day. Okay, so maybe that's not true. Maybe I'd be here regardless, but for the love of God, put me out of my misery and deliver me my damn sex toy. My heart pounds as I repeat that sentence in my head, because I'm already wishing I'd never ordered the stupid thing.

I blame Becca for this.

When I complained to her that she never puts enough thought into my birthday gifts, she presented me with a gift card for Diddle Me Softly. It had been sitting in my drawer for nearly six months. It was only last week when I decided to do a spring clean that I found it. I was all alone in my apartment, so naturally, my mind began to tick over. I'm a twenty-six-year-old single woman with a healthy sexual appetite who was experiencing somewhat of a drought when it came to men. So why did looking at toys and vibrators make me feel so embarrassed? I mean, who was going to know what I got up to in the privacy of my own home? So long as I didn't whip it out in the middle of the subway, I thought it was a pretty safe assumption that nobody would ever know.

One glass of wine was all it took for me to load up that site and have a look.

The first thing that surprised me was the sheer variety of toys available. Was there really that big a market for this kind of thing? Maybe I'd gone into the wrong profession with medicine because obviously sex toy development was the way to go.

As I ran through page after page of toys, I became more overwhelmed and curious at the same time, until I stumbled across the Clitmaster7000. Despite its slightly terrifying name, it actually looked pretty tame compared to some of the other things on offer, so I thought it was a safe option for a beginner like me. I mean, forgive me for being a prude, but the idea of something bigger than my forearm going anywhere near my vagina was *not* getting me all hot and sweaty. So, I took the plunge and ordered it.

I unlock the door and peek outside. A thought hits me as I glance down the hallway and my gaze falls on my neighbor's door. My eighty-year-old widowed neighbor.

God, please don't let it have been delivered to Iris by mistake.

The number of times she brings me my half-opened mail,

because she didn't think to check the name on the label before opening it... Well, I wouldn't put it past her to have signed for my package, opened it up and assumed it was a toy for her cat, Milton. I cringe as I picture him swatting that bad boy from one end of her apartment to the other. I slam the door closed and lean against it.

I cringe because how would I explain that?

I feel like I need to put it all into perspective because I'm probably coming across as that annoying, whiny girl that nobody wants to be friends with. While there may be an element of that, panicky and jumpy isn't who I am.

I'm a doctor, for God's sake. I deal with situations that push me to the edge on a daily basis. I can handle a medical emergency any day of the week, but a situation that I can't control? Even something as simple as a potentially embarrassing package arriving, I struggle with. I'm the first to admit I have flaws and worrying about what other people think of me is probably my biggest.

The knock on the door comes so suddenly that I jump about a meter in the air and nearly give myself a heart attack. *This thing is already trying to kill me, and I haven't even tried it yet.* When the thudding of my heart has subsided, I brush myself off and stroll over to the door, casually opening it like I'm expecting a delivery of toilet paper.

The delivery guy stands there, smiling at me as he cradles the brown wrapped box like it's a new baby. I frown, my paranoia kicking into overdrive. Is he looking at me funny? He glances down at the box in his hands, and then back at me.

"Package for a Lauran Black," he says.

"Laura," I whisper.

I go to snatch it out of his hands and fumble, then we both watch in horror as it falls to the floor—well, I'm horrified; he looks mildly amused.

"Hope there's nothing breakable in there," he says leaning down to pick it up. "Underneath all that brown paper. I always try to guess what little treats people have bought themselves." He winks at me and my heart stops beating. "And you know what they say about brown paper."

God, the delivery guy knows I bought myself a sex toy.

He hands it to me again, along with a form that I quickly sign and thrust back to him. I send him on his way and slam the door closed, leaning up against the door. I slide down it until I'm sitting on the floor, where I carefully examine the box. All I want to do is throw it out, but it's here now, so I might as well take a look.

I carefully peel away the brown packaging and examine the box. With shaking hands, I open it and then reach inside. The size of the box is deceiving because the actual product is small enough to fit on the end of my finger. Which is the whole idea, I guess. I carefully pull it out. I'm both curious and suspicious that this is going to do anything for me. Even so, I *am* starting to wonder if I'm missing out on something—like Becca seems to think I am. Enough that I'm considering taking it for a test drive right now.

I wander into my room and sit down on my bed, carefully inserting the battery. I press the button, giggling like a twelve-year-old when it comes to life in my hands. I shake my head, because Becca would die if she knew what I was about to do. I'm sure she got the gift card, fully expecting me to never use it, but what else am I going do with my Thursday afternoon? I take a deep breath and turn it on, then I slide it onto my finger and dive under the covers.

It's not like I'm going to be broadcasting this on YouTube or anything.

Here goes nothing... *Oh my.*

I groan as it vibrates against me, surprised at how good it actually feels. I bring my knees up and spread my legs a little farther apart, massaging my clit with my new buzzy friend. I clamp down on my lip, stifling a moan as I tease my entrance, pushing my finger just a little farther inside. I gasp, clutching onto the sheet with my other hand as my body begins to react. This is happening faster than I thought it would. I'm ten seconds in and already close to coming. Maybe I *have* been missing out.

"Oh, holy *fuck...*"

I groan, my head snapping back as I thrust it back and forth inside me. I gasp as my hips buck forward and push my finger deeper inside me until I...

My eyes fly open in shock.

Oh no, no, no. Please not this.

I frantically shove my hands out in front of me, like I need confirmation that this is really happening. Because the hands-free buzzing in my vagina isn't a dead giveaway.

Frantically, I try and dig it out, but it's no use. If anything, I think I've made it worse. I groan and grab a handful of sheet as the toy rubs against my clit, driving me crazy.

"Oh lord, fuck, fuck *fuck*," I hiss.

I bite down on my arm to muffle my cries as my heart pounds out of control in my chest. The last thing I need is for Iris to hobble in here to check that I'm okay. Damn me for giving her that key to water my plants while I was away last weekend for my cousin's wedding.

"Oh *God,* make it *stop*."

Gasping, I clench my thighs together, and groan, squeezing my eyes closed. I climax again, number five in as little as ten minutes. The worst thing is, they don't seem to be letting up. If anything, they're becoming more intense. *Oh, my fucking lord.*

I lower myself onto the floor and reach for the box, which has half rolled itself under the bed. My body aches, begging for relief, or at the very least, five minutes where I'm not climaxing. I fumble for the box, dropping it twice, before I get a firm enough grip on it to hold it up to my face. My hands shake as I struggle to read. Then I see those three little words that make me feel like I'm going to pass out.

For external use only.

Who the hell designs a vibrator for external use only? Doesn't that defeat the whole purpose? Am I the only one who thought letting my finger do a little traveling wasn't going to do any harm? Or am I just the only one unlucky enough to have their vagina decide to inhale it? Maybe I should've gone with the forearm sized one, because this tiny little thing is well and truly stuck inside me.

I should call an ambulance.

I laugh, dismissing that as an option. And say what? That's out of the question anyway because of which hospital they would take me to. I'd rather die a slow and painful orgasmic death than be wheeled into the ER of the hospital I'm supposed to be starting work at next week.

Groaning, I fall forward against the bed, fumbling for my phone as another orgasm rips through my body. Sweat covers my forehead as I close my eyes and clench my thighs, my vagina throbbing as I struggle to breathe. Panting, I resume my search for my phone, finally finding it hiding between the pillows. I somehow manage to get Becca's name up on the screen. I sigh, relieved, because this is *not* the time to be calling the wrong number.

"Hello?"

"Get over here." I gasp. "*Now*."

"What? Where are you? What's going on?" she asks.

"Becca," I groan, barely able to focus on what I need to say to her. "Get. Over. Here. *Now*."

"Okay, I'm coming."

Apparently, so am I.

I gasp and drop the phone, crying out as the toy plays me like a violin.

I crawl across the floor in the direction of the living room. She's got to be at least ten minutes away, but that's probably how long it'll take me to get over there. I can barely manage a few slithers at a time because it's at the point where it just *hurts*. The orgasms themselves feel incredible, but those few minutes in between is just pure torture. I'm not sure how much more of this I can take. On top of everything else, I'm completely exhausted. This has to be the most intense work out I've ever had.

Becca pounds on the door just as orgasm number six tapers off. I can barely move by this point, but I made it to the door to unlock it in time and that's the main thing. Now all I need is for her to get this thing out of me.

"It's me," she calls out. "Are you going to let me in?"

"It's open," I manage to gasp.

She walks in, her eyes widening at the sight of me hunched over the couch, thighs clenched, rocking back and forth on the floor. *At least I'm not naked.* I managed to half squirm my way into a dress that I found lying on the floor in my room—though I must look a mess—with only one arm through the hole and the skirt bunched up around my waist. Now that I think about it, I'm not sure why I even bothered. She sprints over to me, crouching down beside me.

"Jesus, are you okay?" She glares at me as I let out a strangled groan. "Tell me what's wrong?" she says. She looks me over, her eyes wide with concern. "Were you attacked? Did someone break in and rape you? Talk to me, Laura. Should I be calling an ambulance?" Her dark eyes study mine as I struggle to form words to answer any of her questions. "For God's sake, Laura. Say *something*."

"No ambulance," I mutter.

I groan and clamp my legs together, gasping as my body begs for relief. This is a nightmare. I point to the bedroom, where the box is still lying on the bed. Becca stalks through to my room, returning a few seconds later with the box in her hands. Her eyes widen, to the point where they're nearly ready to fall out of her head.

"No fucking *way*," she hisses.

I nod, sweat pouring out of places I didn't know sweat could form. She clasps her hands over her mouth and stifles her laughter, before quickly crouching down next to me.

"What do you want me to do? Dig it out? I'll do that for you," she says as I glare at her. "Wait... I should've asked before offering. Front or back?"

"Becca," I growl, my voice high noting at the end.

"What? I'm sorry, it was a legitimate question," she cries, holding her hands up in defense. "You know I don't handle poop. How on earth did you manage to get it stuck in there in the first place?" she asks, shaking her head.

"Can we discuss this later, *after* it's been removed from my vagina?" I beg her.

"Yes, yes, I'm sorry. Okay, let's get you down to my car."

"Car?" I say, alarmed. "What happened to you offering to help me—"

"You seriously want me digging around in there like I'm looking for loose change down the back of the couch?" she asks seriously. Then she giggles, but she stops when she sees my expression. "Sorry. Disturbing mental image. You understand this is pushing the friendship boundaries, right?"

I nod weakly. *Oh, I understand it, all right.*

She sighs and helps me climb up properly onto the couch while I groan as my body begins to convulse. *God, not again.* I wipe a layer of sweat off my forehead and rock back and forth, riding out the orgasm as I whimper into the cushion. Then I gasp, clenching my thighs, until it passes.

"You're coming already? But I haven't even worked my magic hands on you yet," she jokes, flexing her fingers.

"Just get it out," I beg her.

"Fine," she grumbles as she gets down onto her knees. She lifts up the skirt of my dress and peers between my legs. "Hey, you smell really good. What kind of body wash do you use?"

"*Becs.*"

"Right, sorry," she mutters. "Focus."

I close my eyes, my toes curling as she slides a finger inside me. I groan, thrusting my knees together, because just the feel of her fingers inside me is driving me insane.

"This kind of feels like that game we used to play at Halloween, where we had to find the balls in the slime, while blindfolded," she muses.

"Except with less balls," I mutter.

She spends the next half a minute feeling around inside me, then she jumps to her feet and backs up so far, she's standing against the wall on the other side of the room. She shakes her head, a mortified look on her face.

"I'm sorry, I love you, but I can't do this. I can't feel it anyway and what if I damage something or pull the wrong bit out?" she demands.

I laugh, even though I want to cry, because the situation is so helpless. My hands shake as I lift them to my head and cover my face. I'm so tired, and I can already feel another orgasm beginning to develop.

"Do you want me to call an ambulance?"

"*No*."

"Why not?" she asks, surprised by my sharp tone.

"Because they'll take me to Mercy," I say, gritting my teeth.

"Yeah, because it's the closest... *Oh*." She pauses and at least *tries* to fight the smile forming on her lips. "It's also where you start your residency next week. I guess this isn't the kind of first impression you want to make."

"You reckon?" I say, on the verge of tears. "Please, Becs, just *help* me."

She frowns at me. "Can you walk?"

"No," I whisper. "I crawled from the bed to here and it took twenty minutes."

"Then I'll have to carry you." She turns around, bending her knees as she taps her back. "Jump on," she urges me.

"What?" I protest. "I'm two inches taller than you," I say, laughing in spite of how desperate I feel. "You can't piggy back me all the way downstairs—"

"Unless you have a better idea, shut your trap, and get on," she demands. I climb on, wrapping my arms around her neck as I hold on for dear life. "You know, I always dreamed that one day, you'd be having repeated orgasms while riding on my back," she jokes, leading me into the elevator, which, thank God, is empty.

By some miracle, she manages to carry me all the way down to her car, while passing minimal people. I hurl myself across her back seat and whimper. She shuts the door and gets in, glancing back at me with a frown on her face.

"You know, I'm totally regretting getting you that gift card right now," she grumbles.

"Really?" I mutter, gasping as a stab of pain slices through me. *That can't be good.* "Well I think I'm regretting it more."

How did this go so wrong? I picked the least scary looking toy on that damn site. Who could mess that up?

Me. Apparently, I can because here I am vibrating my way to the emergency room, instead of heaven, like I was promised on the box.

I insist we go far enough out of downtown LA that there's no chance of running into anyone I know, and forty minutes later, we're finally nearing the exit for the Orange County Hospital. As Becca takes the exit, the severity of the situation starts to sink in. I feel like passing out. *What the hell am I going to say?* How am I going to explain to a doctor that I, a medical professional, have managed to lodge the world's smallest vibrator inside me?

"Here we are," Becca soothes as she cuts off the engine.

"You wait here; I'm going to race inside and find you a wheelchair."

I nod, resting my head against the seat as she disappears. All the worst possible outcomes are racing through my head right now. What if I need surgery? Forget about the pain or explaining this to a doctor, how I do explain it to Mom and my brother, Matt? I'm such a shit liar, too, so if I concoct some story, they're going to see right through it and badger me until I confess the truth, which pretty much happened with every lie I told during my childhood.

The door opens, and I look up, expecting to see Becca. Instead, I see a middle-aged male orderly smiling sympathetically at me.

"Your friend said you might need some assistance getting out?"

"Thanks," I say, not sure what else to say to that.

Becca's face appears behind him, mouthing I'm sorry. I brace myself and carefully slide my butt across the seat to the door. I groan, my thighs twitching as I bury my face in the seat, pressing my legs together. I sob softly as I come for what feels like the thousandth time.

After this, I don't think I'll ever want to orgasm again.

Of course, I know I'll stop thinking that the moment this is over. It's like gorging yourself with Easter eggs to the point where you're physically sick. You swear off chocolate for life, and it lasts for two hours. Or maybe that's just me.

"There we are," he says as I sit down in the chair. I nod, my heart racing as I lower my head. "Let's get you inside now, hey?"

He hasn't asked what the problem is, which makes me wonder how much Becca told him. Usually orderlies talk your ear off, asking you all sorts of invasive questions. Not this guy, though. This guy is even avoiding eye contact.

He wheels me into a cubicle and helps me onto the bed. I gasp, clutching hold of his arm as the movement triggers another orgasm. They're getting shorter now, which is good, but it's just constant pain. All I can think is how I'm on my knees, clutching some strange man's arm, while he supports me through an orgasm. When he starts trying to soothe me like he's comforting a crying baby, I nearly lose it—in more ways than one.

"You're okay. We'll get you checked out and get this pain under control," he assures me.

I nearly faint with relief. Pain. He thinks I'm in pain.

Oh, thank God for that.

Rolling myself over, I lie back on the bed and smile, my heart pounding erratically in my chest. I close my eyes and focus on my breathing, trying to slow down my heart rate. I find the best position is to lie flat on my back with my legs slightly parted. The less I move, the easier it is to handle, even though there's no relief from the constant discomfort.

I listen to Becca thanking the orderly for his help. I wait until he's gone before I crack open my eyes to see Becca crouching over my face. Her eyes are laced with concern.

"I'm sorry," she whispers. Her usually bright eyes are laced with worry as she clutches my hand. "He insisted on helping when I asked for the chair. I told him you had an exploding cyst."

I laugh at that and even manage a smile.

"It's fine."

She touches my forehead and frowns. "You're sweating bucket loads, Loz. Maybe I should go and find—"

"Please don't." I gasp, clutching her arm. "I want to avoid talking about this for as long as I can." I glance at her, a horrible thought suddenly hitting me. "Actually, can you request a female doctor for me?" I mumble. "I don't think I can handle telling this story to a male."

Especially if he's young and even remotely attractive.

"I'll see what I can do," she promises.

She walks out, leaving me alone as another orgasm hits me. I'm exhausted as I cry out, my hands grabbing hold of the sides of the bed I'm lying on. I groan, my back arching as my body starts to tremble. Finally, it subsides, leaving me breathless and nearing my limit. I wipe my eyes because I'm not sure how much more of this I can handle.

What if they never stop?

"Laura Black."

My head whips around. I stare at the deliciously sexy doctor standing in front of me, staring down at a clipboard. I want to die. My breathing shallows as panic takes over.

Oh God, no.

This guy is perfect in every way. From his well-defined muscles that are peeking out of his scrubs, to his messy, but stylish dark hair, right down to those dreamy, chestnut colored eyes... He looks like a freaking model, and he's *definitely* not someone I want to discuss this with.

Where the hell is Becca with my female doctor?

"Hi. I'm Doctor Dillon, one of the resident doctors here." He smiles warmly at me, but I don't smile back. I'm in too much shock to do anything other than gawk at him like an idiot. He glances down at his clipboard and then back at me. "So, you have an exploding cyst. How bad is the pain, on a scale of one to ten right now?" he asks. "And have you had cysts in the past?" he adds, flicking through his notes.

His brow furrows when I don't answer either question. He steps closer to the bed. I jump, causing my body to react in the one way I don't want it to in front of him. I blink back tears, squirming as I clench my thighs closed while doing my best to ignore him as he looks at me in surprise.

"I can't talk to you. I need a female doctor," I puff, my face flaming.

"I totally get that, Laura. I'm more than happy to request that for you, but we're severely understaffed tonight so you might be waiting a while." He clears his throat. "I can assure you I'm very professional. I take the safety and privacy of my patients very seriously, and I'll do everything I can to make sure you're comfortable."

He speaks earnestly while I lie there, defeated. I know I can't put up with this for much longer. So what if he's hotter than a Calvin Klein model and in five minutes, he'll be elbow deep inside me, probably while I'm in the middle of an orgasm?

As soon as this is over, I never have to see him again. The important thing right now is to get this out of me. I take a deep breath and nod.

"Fine, let's just get it over with," I mutter, gritting my teeth.

"Okay, can you tell me more about the cyst?" he asks. "Has it been diagnosed previously?"

"I..." I swallow, my heart pounding. I close my eyes and force the words out. "There is no cyst. I had a mishap with a toy."

"I'm sorry?" he says, frowning at me. "I don't understand what you—" He stops mid-sentence and stares at me, his eyes widening. "*Oh.*" After a moment of reflection, he quickly moves on. "So, it's stuck? *Inside* your vagina?"

"I wouldn't be here if it wasn't," I snap, close to tears again.

"Right," he replies.

He shakes his head, looking a bit lost at what to do next. Given that he's a resident, this could well be his first disappearing vibrator case. *Yay for being his first.*

"Okay, so have you attempted to get it out?" he asks.

I nod. "I've tried, but I can't get myself into the right position. Every time I do, it triggers an orgasm."

"Do you have a phone?" he asks.

"No, why?" I say.

I have no idea where this is heading. He reaches into his pocket and hands me his phone. I stare at it, confused. Does he want this on video to show his friends later? That doesn't sound very professional to me.

"I want you to google a picture of the toy. When I go in, it will help if I know what I'm looking for," he explains.

He explains it like I've asked him to go to Toys "R" Us on black Friday and he doesn't know what he's looking for. I sigh and snatch his phone from him. I'm past the point of being embarrassed about this. I just want it over with, and if he needs more of a visual than what he's about to get, then I'll give it to him.

"There," I growl, thrusting his phone back to him.

I look up in shock when the curtain is whisked back, and Becca appears.

"There aren't any female..." Her voice trails off as she stares at my doctor. "Oh."

"Hi," he says, frowning at her. "We're kind of in the middle of something here."

"Right, I'm her friend."

She edges closer to me, her eyes growing wide when she catches sight of what's on his phone. I close my eyes and groan.

"This might get fairly invasive," Doctor Dillon says to me. "I'm not sure it's an activity you want your friend here to witness?"

"Oh, trust me, I've had a good old feel around up there." Becca laughs. Her face falls when I glare at her. "Still, I might wait out here, just in case," she whispers, backing up. She gives me a big thumbs-up as she disappears behind the curtain.

He turns back to me, his eyes locking on mine.

"I'm going to examine you if that's okay?"

"Knock yourself out," I say, my voice weak.

Thank God I waxed last week.

Being such a new doctor, I'd only had the one patient experiencing sexual gratification gone wrong, but he was male, and it was a TV remote up his anus, so it wasn't quite the same. I'm not entirely sure what this examination is going to entail, and I'm not looking forward to finding out. Of course, I don't have much choice.

I take a deep breath as he lifts up the gown to reveal my pelvis.

"Okay, let me know if you feel any pain or tenderness." He presses various points, studying my face for my reaction. I shake my head because all the pain and discomfort is much farther south. "No pain at all?" he asks.

"There's not really pain associated with you pressing down," I say, trying to explain what I'm feeling. "It's more constant," I finally say. "And much, much lower."

"That's good news," he says. He smiles encouragingly. "I think I can retrieve it manually without the need for surgery if you're happy for me to try?"

Manually. As in, with his hands. I close my eyes and make peace with the fact that there is no saving this situation. At this point, I might as well roll with the punches and get it over with.

"Sure," I say, a small smile on my lips. "But at least tell me your name before you penetrate me?"

He chuckles at that. "Luke."

He disappears for a moment, then comes back in wearing gloves and carrying a large bottle of lubricant and the biggest set of forceps I think I've ever seen. If I wasn't freaking out before, I certainly am now. Remember what I said about needing to be in control? My heart pounds as he pulls on his gloves and then sets up a wound care kit on the table next to the bed.

"So, how many lost toys have you retrieved?" I whisper, my throat dry.

He glances at me, amused. "Enough to know what I'm doing," he assures me. To me, that translates to none. "I'm going to start with just an internal exam. I promise you, if I'm not confident I can get it by hand, I'll stop and do an ultrasound. Okay?"

I nod, swallowing the baseball sized lump that has formed in my throat. I flinch as he reaches for a speculum and greases it up. He smiles sympathetically at me.

"Any discomfort or if you need a break, just tell me, okay?"

I nod and squeeze my eyes shut, jumping at every tiny touch. *It's just like having a pap smear. There's nothing to be concerned about.*

"I'm going in," he says.

I groan as he slides the instrument into place, gasping as it triggers another orgasm. I've lost count of what number we're up to, but this one feels much more intense. Probably because there is an insanely hot man only inches from my vagina. And in a few minutes, that insanely hot man will be placing his fingers inside me.

Oh god.

Wrong thing to think about. I arch my back slightly, the combination of him and the vibrator pushing me over the edge.

I throw my arm over my mouth, trying to smother my moans. I'm so embarrassed, but apparently, my body doesn't care too much about that. At least, not enough to stop me from climaxing twice in the space of a minute.

Panting, my hands shake as I come down from my high—which is ironically also my lowest point of the day. I feel like crying. I want to get up and run out of here and never look back. The only thing stopping me is that I know I'll get probably as far as the nurse's station before it all starts again.

"Keep as still as you can, Laura. I know this is hard, but I can feel it. I just need to get a little deeper..." I whimper at the thought of anything of his going deeper inside me. "There. Got it."

My eyes fling open. My heart pounds, waiting for the next orgasm to begin, but nothing happens. Still, I brace myself and wait, and... nothing. I smile at him, tears welling in my eyes. I'm not even fazed that he's grinning from ear to ear while holding the buzzing little sucker out in front of him, like it's a prized fish he's just caught.

"Oh, thank God," I gasp. I'm crying like a baby because the relief is incredible. *Now all I need is to sleep for a week, and I'll be fine.* "I can't thank you enough," I add, resisting the urge to hug him. *God, I'm so emotional.*

"You're welcome. I think this is the first time I've ever had a woman be *grateful* that I've stopped her from orgasming," he quips.

"I'm more than grateful. I'm thrilled," I say.

I sit up and swing my legs over the edge of the bed and

stand up. He lunges forward to steady me when I struggle to keep my balance. I wince and rub my stomach. I clearly underestimated how sore I'd be.

"You really shouldn't be leaving yet," he says, frowning at me. "I'd like to keep you in for a few hours, so I can monitor you."

"Thanks, but I really need to get home," I say. All I can think about is getting as far away from here as I can, and I know for a fact that he can't make me stay.

"Okay, well if you insist on going, I can't stop you," he says. He reaches into his pocket and pulls out a script pad, scribbling on it. Then he rips it off and hands it to me.

"So, that's it? There's no other... aftercare needed?" I ask.

"Come back if there's any bleeding or pain, but you should be fine," he assures me. He manages to address me without smirking, but I can see the amusement in his eyes. "You'll be tender for a few days, and you might want to avoid using your toys for a few weeks."

"Damn, however will I cope," I mutter, narrowing my eyes at him.

He probably thinks I've got a kinky dungeon thing going on in my basement.

"Intercourse is fine once the tenderness has eased," he adds, a twinkle in his eyes.

"Trust me, *nothing* will be going near my vagina for a long time," I assure him.

"Sit," Becca insists.

She arms herself with the wheelchair after I've signed all the forms, agreeing that I'm going against doctor's orders by leaving so soon. I'm just thankful this ordeal is finally over.

Much to Becca's surprise I willingly sit down. I'm still quite unsteady on my feet, so I'm all for her wheeling me out of here. Once at the car, she helps me into my seat and heads back into the hospital to return the chair. I breathe out, enjoying the moment to myself. All I have to do is think about what happened, and I die with embarrassment all over again. I think what makes it worse is that I know the kind of shit doctors say about their patients behind closed doors. I'm in that environment every day, where getting a patient like me is like winning the lottery.

Becca climbs in the car slamming the door shut. She takes one look at my face and bursts into laughter. I glare at her, which just makes her laugh even harder. If I had the energy, I'd get out of the car and walk home.

"I'm sorry, but I've been holding that in all day," she splutters. "I know it's not funny, but oh my freaking God, Loz, it could *only* happen to you." She forces the words out through her laughter and tears. "You're the only person I know to visit the ER with a toy lodged inside you. They make shows about people like you. Then, if that wasn't bad enough, you manage to get yourself fingered by the sexiest doctor I've ever laid my eyes on," she says as she shakes her head. "Maybe I need to order myself one of them."

"What he did to me was closer to fisting than fingering." I

scowl at her. "And thank you so much for the rundown, but I'm well aware of what just happened because in case you don't remember, I was there."

She nods furiously. "You're right, I'm so sorry. I'm a terrible friend, but I just had to get it out." She glances at me, biting back either tears or laughter. I'm not sure which. "I'm sure you know what that's like, right?"

She erupts into another wave of giggles, while I glare straight ahead.

"Are you done?" I snap.

"I think so," she mumbles. She takes a deep breath and straightens herself up. She looks at me, trying to disguise her grin as sympathy. "At least you don't have to see him again, right?" she points out.

Thank God for that.

Get your copy!

ABOUT THE AUTHOR

A New York Times and USA Today bestselling author, Missy lives in a small town in Victoria, Australia with her husband and her confused pets (a dog who thinks that she is a cat, a cat who thinks he is a dog...you get the picture).

When she's not writing, she can usually be found looking for something to read.

Visit her website or subscribe to her newsletter for updates.

facebook.com/MissycJohnson

twitter.com/missycjohnson

instagram.com/authormissyj

amazon.com/Missy-Johnson

bookbub.com/authors/missy-johnson

ALSO BY MISSY JOHNSON

Love Hurts Series

Always You

Out of Reach

Words Left Unsaid

Don't Hold Back

Fade to Black

Awkward Love Series

It's Complicated

I Can Explain

Too Much Information

Comfort Zone

Don't Go There

Standalones

Rewriting History

Resist

Absolution

Printed in Dunstable, United Kingdom

68062114R00170